THE
FOUNTAIN

PATRICIA OLSON

Mom and Kerry, this is for you.

CHAPTER 1

It's a fountain, not a castle tower.

The picture is faded and one of the corners is bent. It looks like a freestanding medieval castle tower built of softball-sized fieldstones, wider at the bottom, and gently curved out at the top. A band about two feet thick made up of smaller stones lines the top. Based on the trees next to it, I think it's about six feet high. I set the photo down on my desk beside the picture that I found online. I compare differences from when it was built to today.

Let's see. It was built in about 1935, so it's about eighty-five years old. And of course, now there's graffiti on it. It looks in good structural shape, though.

My tower is real.

I've dreamt about a stone tower with water flowing from it for years. A simple tower, with no spires or flags or window slits. Just a stone tower with flowing water. I have a lot of dreams. The dreams increase when I'm stressed, anxious, or scared. The tower dream was the only one that reoccured.

I don't see the tower in my sleep anymore.

My name is Sellis. I have a great life here in western

North Dakota. I run a nursery with my husband, Caleb, and daughter, Lily. I work hard and have time to laugh and play with the people I love.

I've researched castles, towers, and dream symbolism for years, so I'm a little embarrassed. I enjoyed the mystical aspects associated with a recurrent dream about a castle tower. Maybe I had royal blood mixed in with my Midwestern roots. Who knew?

I pick up the picture and head down the hall to the kitchen.

I found it in a box of my mom's old letters, photographs, and newspaper clippings that my younger sister, Kate, sent me earlier this month. I finally sat down and went through the box last week. I didn't recognize faces in the pictures and had no idea who these people were, though some of them had Mom's maiden name written on the back. I went through the box in the hope I'd recognize someone or find some reason for Mom to have kept them.

I came across one that gave me a jolt. Two women, with their arms around each other, laughing into the camera. Faded writing on the back said, "Sophie and Flossie 1954." I don't think I'd ever seen a picture of my mom when she was so young. I never saw my mom laugh like that. And was that my Grandma Flossie? Oh. My. Gosh.

I'd set their picture aside and glanced through a couple of the letters. Most were to Sophie from Flossie with a return address of Crystal Springs, North Dakota. And then, almost at the bottom, I found the picture of the fountain.

It was a key. A key that unlocked a hidden door I'd

forgotten. Memories and snippets of stories about Crystal Springs flickered through my mind.

I had been there. I had seen the fountain.

I trace the outline of the fountain in the picture before I put it in a baggie. I remember more each time I look at this picture. I brew myself a cup of tea and look out the window over the sink.

I don't know why our visits to Crystal Springs stopped. Mom told Kate and me she couldn't go there anymore.

When we asked again, she shut down. Went to her bedroom and locked the door. No eating. No talking. No being Mom.

We learned to avoid situations that upset her, and we didn't ask anymore.

Over the years, she'd mention people or friends she said lived there, and it sounded like an established community. I had to grow up. As an adult, I recognize the hidden nuances. There was something different about Mom when she talked about Crystal Springs. She was content and light-hearted. Again, we learned not to ask too many questions, though, because she'd get agitated.

Mom had been mentally ill.

Even now, I stumble sometimes when I try to find the right words to explain what she'd been like. When I was a kid, the closest term we ever used was "sick." Mom was "sick" again.

Life would be okay for a while. Then, with no warning, it wasn't. Sometimes it was being awakened at three in the morning so she could wash our bedding. Or we'd get called to the school office because Mom was there to pick us up, and off we'd go.

When I saw the fountain, I knew we'd gone to Crystal Springs. I don't remember how often we went, but there was a pull there for Mom. A reason she needed to go there.

She died last year, and while I do believe she's finally at peace, I feel like I've overlooked something significant.

The Crystal Springs I know about today is a ghost town. Google tells me it never amounted to much. I think Mom went to *another* Crystal Springs. A different one than the few buildings I've seen from the Interstate. The fountain is part of the mystery. And maybe there's more to Mom's story than her mental illness.

I take a last sip of my tea and set down my cup. I tidy the piles on the island and glance at the paper before I fold it up.

All of my protective mechanisms disappeared when I saw the picture. I must go see the fountain and Crystal Springs and perhaps find some answers.

I'm a modern-day knight on a quest with her faithful steed, or in my case, my Triumph motorcycle.

Serviced and clean, the chrome sparkles, and the gas tank is full. The only thing left to do is pack the saddle bags on the bike. My granddaughter, Emma, is coming along so I'm curious to see how her packing is going.

Emma is nine-years-old, and we get to spend a lot of time together. She lives in town with her mom, Lily, but also has her own room here. This will be her first motorcycle road trip and our last big adventure of the summer.

Barks and giggles erupt from the garage, so I head

out there. Emma straddles the "Trumpet" - my Triumph motorcycle. Both feet are planted on the passenger pegs. Caught up in her excitement, my two dogs circle the bike in a flurry of tail wags and enthusiastic barks.

Emma looks over her shoulder at me. Her eyes are hidden behind her black sunnies with pink neon pawprints on the bows.

"Nice touch." I grab the bike key off the wall.

On her lap is the helmet she finished last night. The original black is barely visible under the pink leopard print she added.

I push the garage door opener. "Okay, Em, move those long legs, and get your backpack. Don't forget to call your mom."

She puts her helmet on and throws her arms out in a Vanna White pose. "What do you think, Gram?"

"I love it."

Off the bike, she hugs me and dashes into the house with the dogs close behind. Her stream of conversation continues with Caleb added to the mix. I hear the ebb and flow of their voices through the open windows. The excitement in her high pitched voice is offset by Caleb's low, calm tones. "Have you ever been to Crystal Springs? Did you know there was a fountain there? Did you know my grandma Sophie? I don't remember her, but my mom does. How cool is it that we're finally going on our road trip? And then, school starts." His actual responses are covered up by her chattering.

I grab hold of the handgrips and straighten up the Trumpet. I lift my right leg over the seat, sit down, and smile. My Trumpet fits me like a well-worn pair of jeans. I roll the bike out of the garage.

For a moment, I sit and look out over the yard. Beads of dew glisten on the grass, and the sun peeks over the trees beside Willow Creek. Ducks and geese float past. Geese honk, squirrels scold, and magpies chatter. It's the start of another day.

"Please keep us safe," I ask the universe.

Back in the kitchen, Caleb hands me my cup. "Here's one for the road. It's a good thing you know where all the restrooms are in the state," he says with a wink.

"Thanks," I reach and pull out his collar, "I think."

"Are you planning to superglue Emma to the seat?"

"I wish I could run the bike off her energy." I tug his beard. "By the way, I like the salt and pepper look, husband."

"Some people would call me distinguished. Now that you've stopped moving, there's a ton of energy sparkling around you, too." He sets my cup down and wraps his arms around me. "I hope you find answers and ease your heart. You two go and have fun while Lily and I take care of things." He rests his chin on my forehead as he holds me.

"Turnabout is fair play, husband. How many times do I stay at home while you go play?"

He laughs as he goes outside with the dogs close behind.

In our bedroom, I check my backpack one last time. T-shirts, jeans, pj's, tennies to wear when I take off my boots: I'm done.

My phone bings.

"ride safe, cu nxt wk, love u" A text from Lily, Emma must have called her mom.

I braid my hair and grab my "WindTrees Nursery" hat. Thank goodness for braids and hats. Caleb's not the only one getting gray around here. No longer a biker chick, I've become a granola grandma.

And one that's gonna need sunscreen.

I grab the sunscreen and some extra hair ties and stuff them in next to my current read. Can't leave home without a book.

Grabbing my leather jacket from the hall closet, I check to make sure my gloves are in the pockets. *I bet Emma's already got hers on.* My hand hovers over my bird bag, and I decide yes. Who knows? Maybe Tawny, the owl, will follow me. I want to be prepared.

CHAPTER 2

Bike packed, I'm ready. Emma can't stand still. *Caleb's right. I wonder if she'll be able to sit still on the bike?* She hops from one foot to the other, her arms wrapped around her waist.

I start the Trumpet, and it responds with its soft, distinctive growl. "Put your helmet on, Em. Let's go."

I tighten my helmet strap and put on my gloves while Caleb helps Emma finish. She moves so fast once her helmet's on, she looks like she's flying. "Step on the footpeg and lift your leg over the seat."

"I know, Gram, I know," she says as she puts her hand on my shoulder and steps up. Settled in, she wraps her arms around my waist.

"Let's roll!"

Caleb and I smile at each other. This has been her catch-phrase this summer whenever we go for a ride. He leans over for a quick kiss. I shift into first, and we're on our way.

At the end of our driveway, we turn left and follow the road and creek into the sun.

We cruise along the curves of Old Highway 10. It feels so darn good to be on my bike. I smile at Emma's reflection in my mirror as she squeezes my waist. I don't know who's more excited: her or me.

We ride past herds of cows and sheep and orchards and grain fields. It smells like apples and home. I breathe in the sweet, familiar aroma. Harvest is in full swing now and should be finished before the autumn rains begin.

The sun feels warmer as we head east. The curves of the old highway take us to the Interstate which stretches in front of us like a long, straight ribbon. Emma relaxes as the miles go by. I can't hear her, but I know when she's relaxed, she sings and taps her fingers to keep time. I feel the movements of her loosely draped fingers. This makes me one happy grandma.

The day is perfect. Sunny with barely any wind. I'm glad we got an early start. We've been able to stop and walk around and savor our ride. We make a couple of stops for gas, and thanks to Emma (and my Trumpet), they've been fun. There are Triumph riders everywhere, and like most bikers, they have stories to share. Part of the joy of riding is the people we meet.

"My gram has been riding for years. She rides every-where, even to church. I'll probably end up with her bike when she's too old to ride anymore." Who is this cool little chick up at the counter at the Coffee Cup Fuel Stop when I come in from filling gas? The clerk looks over at me and winks.

"What year is the Trumpet, Gram? I can't remember." *Oh my gosh, she is too funny.*

"It's a 2001 Bonneville America."

"This lady is Francine. Her dad had a Triumph, too. I think it's older than yours, though."

9

The landscape changes the farther east we go. No longer quite as flat, these bigger hills are covered with grain ready to be harvested like at home. We pass slow-moving farm machinery that lumbers along on the Interstate.

It's early afternoon when we reach the Crystal Springs exit. We turn off. "Is that it? It's so cool." Emma points to the huge white sign with the words Fiddlehead Fern Bed & Breakfast surrounded by green, ornate ferns. I pull into the empty driveway alongside the two-story house, stop the Trumpet, and turn it off. The quiet is a shock after the hours of bike and road noise.

Emma hops off the bike and takes a couple of steps. I loosen my helmet strap and take it and my gloves off.

"My butt hurts. What is that about?"

"Welcome to the wonderful world of motorcycling, Emma. You'll be fine once you walk around a bit."

I get off and open the saddlebag. I pull up the lid and see a black and white kitten tucked in between my backpack and hat. Our kitten, Spike, gazes up at me.

"Spike! How did you get in there?" The latest addition to our family, he's a rescue tuxedo kitten about six months old.

"Purrr" is the response I get as he nudges his head into my hand while I stare at him.

"What? Spike?" Emma whirls around from removing her helmet and gloves, and darts over to me. "Cool, a stowaway. He needs a helmet, Gram."

"Maybe we can find a tennis ball and hollow it out, huh?"

How did he get in the saddlebag?

I pick him up and snuggle him under my chin before I hand him to Emma. I pull out my backpack and hat and set them on the seat beside my helmet. I slip my hat on over my helmet-smushed hair with a quick check in the side mirror. *Whatever, woman. You ride a bike, don't worry about it.* Time to check-in. I hope they allow animals.

CHAPTER 3

Much to my relief, the Fiddlehead's owner, Cindy, doesn't have a problem with her extra guest. In fact, she even helps me rig up a harness and leash with clothesline, and gives us a baggie of her cat's food and two small plastic bowls.

We're the only guests here. We've got a room at the top of the stairs with a full-sized bed and a twin covered with matching quilts and piles of pillows. There's a nightstand with a reading lamp beside each bed. A vase overflowing with prairie lilies and blanket flowers sits on top of a wooden bookcase beside an overstuffed chair. The room is bright with afternoon sunshine.

"The tub is huge, and it has feet. Can I take a bath tonight, Gram?" Emma explores while I unpack, and Spike soaks up the rays on top of the pillows.

I pick up my journal and flip through the pages. The fountain picture falls out onto the bed. *I'm scared. No, I'm not. I'm nervous. Why have I been dreaming about this fountain? Did I really see it before? Were we really here before? What is the connection to Mom?* I take a deep breath and slowly exhale. *Just breathe, Sellis. This is a simple thing. Just gonna check out a fountain, have a nice ride with Emma. Oh yeah, and Spike. It's not a big deal.*

Settled in, road dust washed off, we head downstairs. Cindy calls us into the kitchen, and we chat about supper. She's not familiar with Mom or Grandma Flossie's names. "I haven't been here that long, though. Maybe those brochures on the buffet in the dining room will help."

I'm on the back steps, and Emma and Spike are sprawled on the grass. Emma's on her back with Spike on her stomach. His contented purrs and her soft murmurs float along the edges of my thoughts.

I read that the Fiddlehead B&B is part of the original town. They built the Interstate in the early 1960s, and it literally split the town in half, leading to its demise. There are pictures of the town that make me think about Mom's letters. I bet if I could find a map of the original town, I could find the address listed on them. In my journal, I find the directions to the lake where the fountain is located. It's a few miles away, but it shouldn't be hard to find.

"What's the name of that song Gramps likes about the magic carpet? You know, he says that's what it feels like when he's on his motorcycle. I want to tell him I sang it today for him."

"Magic Carpet Ride," I respond.

Which reminds me, how in the heck did Spike get in my bag?

Seriously, someone had to have put him in there, and I know it wasn't Emma. She was as shocked as I was. I know that girl too well and would have known if she had done it. Like me, she's an open book. The look of delight on her face was spontaneous and sincere.

Caleb? No, he's too practical. He'd have too many reasons why a kitten on a bike trip wouldn't work.

Maybe Spike is, like Emma says, a magical cat. Of course, I don't know what she's basing that on, other than his extreme cuteness and playfulness.

We call Caleb and fill him in on our adventures and agree to check in with him tomorrow when we get to the fountain. "Gramps says he didn't pack Spike." *So who did?*

It's dusk and beginning to cool down. We eat and go for a walk. We're in the back yard while Spike chases fireflies. Crickets and bird calls fill the occasional quiet spaces.

All of a sudden, Spike dashes across the yard and up onto the porch.

"What's wrong?" Emma asks as she scoops him up.

Branches quiver in one of the poplars lining the yard. "Tawny, is that you?"

I hear soft hoots as I walk over to the trees. When I look up, I glimpse the brown owl peering down.

CHAPTER 4

Tawny, the great horned owl, followed us.

Emma and Spike snuggle under my arm as we look up at her and beam at each other.

"Who are you, Tawny? Hoo Hoot Tawny," Emma calls as she holds Spike up to wave.

I continue to be amazed at the magical gift of this bird in my life.

Five years ago, in early winter, I spotted a massive nest in the bare trees in a shelterbelt on my drive to town. Then, I saw an owl sitting in it. A great horned owl with very distinctive ear tufts.

I learned the owls' courtship period is in late fall, and eggs are generally laid sometime in December or January. This was inconceivable to me, a native North Dakotan. It's winter. There are blizzards and wind chills of thirty below zero at times. What kind of creature courts, falls in love and has babies in a nest for heaven's sake, in those conditions? Owls. Specifically, great horned owls.

This discovery was an unconventional and sweet treatment for my winter blues.

As far as I know, the same couple occupied the nest

each year. I would watch for the ear tufts, count down approximate gestation times, and wait to see owlets. And pray that the owl family would survive our brutal winters. I had some spectacular sightings and moments of joy and delight over the years, beginning with tuft sightings and culminating with owlets.

I have a decent camera with a good zoom, which gave the owls space while allowing me to see them up close. I am always respectful and keep my distance.

It's been just over a year since Tawny became a member of our family.

Last year, I discovered I could access the nest from the other side of the shelterbelt. There's an undeveloped grassland there where I could bring my dogs and let them run while doing some owl gazing. The dogs and I get exercise, and my photo opportunities expand.

There were two owlets, and I was able to get detailed, close-up pictures of them branching and bobbing and hopping.

My nearer presence did not go unnoticed by Mom and Dad Owl. They flew off if we got too close, and a couple of times, one of them swooped my way. Their vigilance and watchful ways kept me mindful, and I did my best to not get too close. Daisy, my lab cross, and Dakota, the Corgi mix, spent time exploring and savoring all of the new and exciting smells, and I worked on my long-range camera skills.

One afternoon, the dogs ran up to a tree and began fiercely barking and growling. Daisy was in full search mode. If she physically could have, she would have climbed that tree. As it was, she was stretched up as far as she could.

"Daisy. Dakota. Get down!"

When I got there and looked up, I saw a fluffy, hissing, clicking fuzzball about the size of a volleyball. It was perched on a branch, backed up against the tree trunk, while my two unmannered beasts did their best to climb up to greet (or eat?) it. The owlet was one of the cutest things I've ever seen.

"Behave and back off!" I grabbed their collars and pulled them away.

I didn't see Mom and Dad owl anywhere; and when I thought about it, I hadn't for a while. The owlet would be about six to seven months old now. Which meant it was weaned and strong enough to be on its own. It didn't seem hurt, so I figured the best course of action was to keep moving.

"Sorry, Owlet." Not wanting to scare it any more, I apologized as we walked away.

"Heel." Finally the dogs training kicked in.

There was a swoosh as the owlet flew past. Okay. That dilemma's solved. Maybe the dogs disturbed it's sleep, and now it could resume its routine. We continued our walk, then headed home without any additional contact.

After that, it seemed like I saw the owlet more. Like it was watching for us.

Then one day, it followed us home.

It flew behind us, sometimes visible as only a speck in my rearview mirror, but always in sight. When we got home, I watched it fly to a branch in one of the poplars along the creek.

I followed the dogs to Caleb's shop to let him know about our visitor.

"Whatever, woman! Next time you'll tell me a miniature burro just happened to follow you home."

"Seriously, Caleb," I insisted, "It's up at the house in the wind trees. The tractor you're working on isn't going anywhere. Come see. This will make you smile."

Daisy and Dakota, of course, keep us company during the short stroll across the yard.

"Ta da!"

"Huh. It really did follow you."

"So, now what?" I asked.

"Well, I'm certainly not going to tell you to bring it in the house like I did when we found Bendigo, the cat, on the front tire of our car." Caleb smiled over at me, then looked back up at the owlet.

"Wait, you're not giving me the choice of either bringing it in the house and feeding it, or taking it out into the shelterbelt?"

We'd had this discussion years earlier when a stray kitten being chased by our dogs took refuge on a tire of one of our cars. I coaxed it out. While I was holding the shivering, yet purring little beast, I asked what we should do. Bendigo joined our household and grew up to be a magnificent, treasured member of our family.

"Nope. We'll just let it be and see what it does," he said. "Crazy. I have never heard of such a thing." I had never heard of such a thing either.

And so it was that Tawny, the owl came to live in our wind trees.

At first, I worried about our cats becoming owl snacks, but she never bothered them. When she's around, I get good morning hoots when I go out with the dogs.

Sometimes there'll be a fly by to let us know she's home in the early morning hours or after dusk. She sits in the birch tree near the house when we're on the porch or perches on the garage roof when we have bonfires. When I hear nighttime hoots from the big, old cottonwood trees by the creek, I like to think they come from Tawny.

It's like she's my guardian angel.

While charmed and a bit besotted with this glorious creature, I'm respectful and continue to learn all that I can. In no way do I consider Tawny an ordinary pet. She's a wild creature that's decided to be part of our world, and I will revel in that as much as possible without overstepping or causing harm.

I started reading about falconry. Because Tawny will fly to me, I had a glove made to protect myself from her talons, which can be unintentionally lethal. Even though she's still young, she's stronger than I'll ever be.

I believe a teacher or the opportunity to learn more will turn up. There aren't any falconry schools in the Midwest, but there are in Scotland. At castles. Where they also have men in kilts. I think that would be a great option.

I hadn't known if Tawny would travel with me. She follows me quite often at home, and instinctively knows when to stop or turn back. However, she's never accompanied me this far before, so this is new territory in more ways than one. I've never clocked her speed, but supposedly owls can fly up to forty miles per hour. When she can't keep me in sight, she soon catches up.

Seeing her here makes my heart dance. I'm comforted by her presence for some reason.

"Sleep tight Tawny, hoot hoot," Emma sings.

I give her a little salute before Emma, Spike, and I head into the house for supper and sleep.

CHAPTER 5

I can't see my breath, but it doesn't feel like summer this morning. In fact, it's downright brisk. I'm glad I checked the forecast so we can wear layers.

"Are these for boys? Why are they called long johns? Do people really wear them for underwear?"

"They're generic. Both men and women can wear them. I don't know why they're called long johns, I bet your grandpa will know, though. Trust me, you'll be glad you have them on. When we're going fifty miles an hour, and it's chilly like it is this morning, it feels a lot colder, and you want as much protection as you can get. Here, see if these fit."

Adjusting her new gauntlets over the sleeves of her jacket, she walks over to me. "Cool. They're just like yours," she says while holding up her hands to show me.

The sun is peeking over the horizon as we tighten our helmets, and I start the Trumpet.

Emma sets Spike into the nest she has made for him in the saddlebag, closes the lid, and fastens the latches. Then she double-checks to make sure he's secure.

We're heading to the lake that Crystal Springs is named for, which is a few miles further east of the B&B.

Back in the 1930s, it was a pleasant stop on Highway 10, which at that time was the main road across the south part of the state. You could buy gas and bait at the local service station. A special treat was a drink from the artesian well located nearby. The water had the reputation of being some of the best tasting for hundreds of miles. For many years people obtained the water through an iron pipe that came from the spring. In 1935 a local stonemason built a fountain with funds from the Works Progress Administration program.

And then progress drove up. When Interstate 94 was built in the 1950s and 1960s, it literally split Crystal Springs in half.

As we're driving, I think of Grandma Flossie's letters and I recall her mentioning the fountain. *What did she say about it? I know I saw the word fountain a few times.* Now that I'm thinking about it, I can remember Mom talking about the fountain, too. That seems odd. What was so special about a fountain? So what if the water was sweet.

Grandma Flossie is part of my story, part of who I am, and part of the reason we're heading down this road in the middle of nowhere. This ghost town was home to her in the prime of her life. Although I knew her as Grandma Flossie, she was actually my great-grandma.

My memories of her are only of a stereotypical "Grandma" type person. I don't think there are many of them around these days. Take me, for example. In my memories, she's in a dress or skirt and blouse. Nylons, of course, and a light tan cardigan that would be draped over her kitchen chair when she wasn't wearing it. Grandma Flossie always wore dresses or skirts. Always. I never knew her as anyone but my elderly grandma.

I just remembered a picture in one of my photo albums of her and my daughter Lily. It's from Grandma's 105th birthday party. Mom, Kate, Lily, and I were there. This was a big deal for a lot of reasons. Living to be 105 years old, of course, but my family get-togethers were few and far between at this point in my life. It had been years since I'd seen Grandma, and I'm sad to admit, I hadn't seen Mom for a while either. We all met up at the nursing home in a small town in the southeast corner of the state. Lily was three years old, yet Grandma Flossie didn't seem much larger than her. In retrospect, I wonder if she was always so small. Lily wore her favorite yellow sweater, and her curly sun-bleached hair is pulled on top of her head in her usual "Pebbles" hair-do. She's snuggled up next to Grandma, who's also wearing a cardigan, and has her hair in a bun. The fact that Lily met her great great grandma is mind-boggling.

Emma's fingers tapping the beat to a song on my waist brings me back to here and now. I'm delighted at how well she's doing riding behind me. She moves with me on the curves; she's the perfect passenger. I know she's comfortable and secure when she's keeping time, rather than having both hands clasped on my waist.

The road rolls along, following the undulating hills. We pass harvested fields and shelterbelts and orchards. I haven't, aside from flocks of birds, seen any other vehicles or signs of life. It's calm; but as the sun rises higher, I feel a slight breeze from the southwest. The sky is clear. I hope there's no rain blowing in. I hate riding in the rain.

Scanning the road and ditches ahead, I keep an eye out for deer and any other creatures who are also waking up and starting to move around.

In the distance, I see the brick schoolhouse. Nudging Emma's left hand with my elbow, I get her attention and nod my head forward.

"Is that the school, Gram? Yay, we're almost there." She wriggles on the seat. "Good, I need to move; my butt is sore."

"Mine too, Em," I nod in agreement.

The road into Crystal Springs is little more than an overgrown path. The church is more gray than white, and no glass remains in any windows. Now that we're closer, I see foundations partially hidden in the broom grass that's overtaken the town. I drive to the front of the old school, stop the bike on a relatively flat spot, and turn it off.

"Okay, Em, go ahead and hop off."

Standing up on the pegs, she effortlessly jumps off and immediately goes to Spike's bag and unbuckles it. Once I remove my helmet and gauntlets, I take Spike from her. As soon as his harness is on, he leaps down and scurries for the tall grass.

Emma chases after Spike. I take out my journal, close the saddlebags and lean against the bike.

I close my eyes and take a breath. And then another. Opening my eyes, I look up.

A few long streamers of clouds blown in with the breeze float high in the sky. Lowering my gaze, I smile at the wind trees scattered around the school. The leaves are starting to turn. I have the feeling there will be more leaves on the ground than on branches by the time the wind is done blowing today.

I breathe deeply, and smell crunchy, autumn leaves, and that bare-branch woody scent that accompanies it.

I pull an envelope out of my journal. Inside is a hand-drawn map of the cabins around the lake that I found in one of Grandma's letters. The ink is faded and hard to decipher in spots. I wish there were directions because the cabins are all gone, so it takes me a moment to orientate myself. Plus, there are a lot more trees now, and the lake is so much bigger due to...

Oh my gosh. What if the lake engulfed the fountain?

I honestly never considered that possibility until now. There are so many things about our world and climate changes that I've adjusted to, and now take for granted. It was a different world back when this map was drawn.

This was plains country then. Grain crops such as wheat, oats, and barley were the primary source of income for many, and the only trees here were planted by farmers for shelter-belts. After years of slowly rising temperatures and increasing rainfalls, the climate gradually changed. Years of too much rain and dams breaking caused overland flooding. Now we're living surrounded by trees and lakes and different varieties of foliage more suited to this new climate. Apple orchards like the ones in my nursery and grapevines fill the hills and valleys that used to be covered by wheat fields. Cottonwood, poplar, and pine trees border newly formed creeks and enlarged lakes.

"Oh, no, no, no. Please let it be there," becomes my mantra as I go to find Emma and Spike.

"Hooo. Hoot." A swoosh over my head bids for my attention. I look up as Tawny flies past and lands in a nearby wind tree.

"Good morning, Tawny." Emma runs over to her and looks up into the tree. "How was your flight?"

Spike saunters over and plops down on his back and does his stretch-and-roll move. Kneeling next to him, Emma automatically rubs his belly while continuing to chat with Tawny.

CHAPTER 6

In case there's no longer a road to it, I fix the fountain's location in my head, and we put our helmets and gloves back on. Spike readily goes back into his little nest, and we head out with Tawny flying overhead.

We leave Crystal Springs, and now we're on a gravel road. It's rough and rutted and slow going. I pull over when we get to the top of a hill. Based on the map, the fountain should be right down there. Yep. I see the fountain down at the bottom, surrounded by brush. There's a trail leading to it, but no road. The road we're on must go to where the cabins used to be.

"Gram, I see it," Emma's voice is shrill. Her hands rest on my shoulders as she stands on the footpegs to look.

"Me, too. Hold on, we're going down."

We're off the bike and Spike's leash is attached in no time at all. Tawny flies by as we walk up to the fountain.

It's beautiful. It looks as though it came from another time and place. I'm enamored.

The fieldstone is weathered, and the colors are muted. It resembles a miniature stone tower. It's about eight feet tall and five feet in diameter. A band of stones about a foot and a half deep rim the top, with the body made up of smaller ones as it curves to the ground. I can't help but touch it. The stones are smooth and cool against my hand.

"Smile for Gramps, Emma. He'll be excited that we're here." I take a quick picture with my phone.

Tawny lands on the edge of the fountain. On the other side, through more trees, I see the lake. The ground slopes down to a sandy beach, and Crystal Springs Lake.

Whoa. That's how close it came to being underwater.

Spike walks up to the fountain, sniffs it, and goes around to the other side. He stretches up on his back legs to bat at the spigot as Tawny peers down at him.

"Well, Emma, do you want to see if it still works?"

She bends down and fiddles with the handle. "I can't turn it, Gram. Can you help me, please?"

My hand covers hers when I reach down. We pull together, and with a jerk, it comes up. A gush of water flows out. Spike leaps away from the downpour, shakes, and immediately starts to groom himself. We laugh at Spike's nonchalance as we back up too. Tawny is now perched with her wings spread like she's ready to take off.

"We need to taste this to see if it's as good as the stories claim." With a step back, I cup my hands under the water. After Emma does the same, and we've both had a drink, I flip the handle down and shake the remaining drops from my hands.

"It is kinda sweet and really cold," Emma pronounces as she picks up Spike. "Now what, Gram? We found the fountain, and it still works. What's next?

The hair on my neck stands up, and I command my

heart to slow down. I'm holding my breath, and as I inhale, I smell ozone.

The landscape has changed. The trail we just used is now a dirt road lined by full-grown trees. What previously was a grassy hill is covered with trees.

My thoughts are jumbled and swirl as I try to make sense of what I see. We are clearly not in the same place we were in before we pulled up the spigot. Maybe, just maybe, Mom wasn't crazy? Perhaps there really is another Crystal Springs? Oh. My. Gosh. Is this really happening?

Tawny flaps her wings a couple of times before she flies off. Spike meows and leaps out of Emma's arms.

"Gram, what's going on?" Emma grabs my hand and steps closer as we look around.

Not only are there more trees, but they're mature, tall, thick, and gnarled. The grass is tall and abundant, and the lake is vast. The air even feels different, dense, and moister somehow.

"Toto, I don't think we're in Kansas anymore." It comes out before I realize Emma is not going to understand my reference, or think I'm funny.

"We're fine, Em. Just breathe." I put my arms around her. "We talked about this, remember? There's a mystery surrounding the fountain, and we're here to try to figure it out. Everything is going to be all right."

Just breathe, Sellis. Listen to what you just told Emma. This is really happening.

Spike is now stalking blades of grass. He's not anxious. Tawny has flown to a nearby tree and is gazing down at us in her inscrutable owl way. I trust their animal senses. If they're not nervous, why should I be?

"Let's go check out the lake, okay? I don't know yet what just happened, but we're on an adventure. I'll always take care of you, Emma. Never, ever forget that."

Her green eyes glisten, and she studies me before she nods. She wraps her arms around me and squeezes tight.

"Okay," she says as she lets go and takes off after Spike.

My heart pounds as I watch her. *Seriously. Sellis, get your act together.* I clasp my hands together, I don't need them to shake in front of Emma. *Think. Stay focused.* I reach for my phone to take pictures and document this. No bars, no signal, nothing. *That's strange. I took a picture of Emma and Spike and sent it to Caleb, what, ten minutes ago? Ohhhh, right. That was before we turned on the water.*

I head down to the lake, and with each step, I'm certain we're no longer in the same place we were twenty minutes ago. Something changed. Something happened. I rein in my racing thoughts and pull out the spirited, adventurous Gram persona.

"Where are we, Gram?" I catch up with Emma and take her hand, matching my steps to hers. Looking up, she blurts, "I'm kinda freaking out."

As though he knows that his people are anxious, Spike saunters up to Emma. She reaches down and picks him up without losing a step, and I hear purrs that feel like hugs.

"Ah, sweetie. I'm not sure what's going on. I can't explain it yet. Spike and Tawny aren't afraid, and I trust their instincts. I'm not scared."

"Remember when we talked about coming here, and I told you it was a mystery trip? Sometimes, there isn't a simple explanation for the things that happen. Things can be complex and scientific." My response is slow and calm as I consider how to explain this. "Like Meg and her search for her dad in the Wrinkle books, remember?" I smile because I know she'll get the connection.

She's an old soul blessed with a quick mind. We've had a two-person book club for the last year and shared many of the books her mom and I read together. The "Wrinkle in Time" series is one of our favorites. Far smarter in math than I am, Emma was intrigued by the scientific parts of the story.

Her voice is pinched and breathy as her words tumble out. Her hands fly out above her head. "It's like everything is bigger, and there's more of it. The trees are gigantic. The lake is huge, and the air feels different. But we didn't go anywhere. We didn't move at all. How did that happen? Can things like this happen to real people? Are we going to find our way home?" Her voice trails off as we get closer to the lake.

There is no resemblance between this lake and the one we pulled up to. This is a significant body of water lying beyond the sandy beach. To my right, a line of boulders extends into the water. They would be perfect for climbing and exploring. I bet a lot of fishing is done from them.

I can barely see the opposite shoreline. What I do see is hilly and covered with trees. I wonder how big this lake is. The breeze that accompanied us on our ride is stronger here, and there are swells on the water. The sound of water slapping against rocks and onto the beach is calming in a seaside sort of way. The air smells salty. Is that because this lake originates from an artesian spring? Isn't that supposed to be salty? *Aaargh*. I don't know what to think.

"Hey, Em. Where do books and stories come from?

Not everything is make-believe. Most of the time, stories are based on something real. That's what we're here to find out. I think there are two Crystal Springs, and it looks like we found the other one." My voice is light. I tug her braid. "C'mon. Race me to the water."

I walk along the big boulders while Emma crouches on the beach, sorting through rocks. Spike investigates the wavelets. He does a sideways scamper over to me as I look out at the water. When he begins to jump from rock to rock, I'm reminded of another cat, another body of water, another lifetime ago.

That was a long time ago. And here I am again with another cool cat and another large body of water.

"Hey, Emma, you know how you call me Gram and Gram Cracker? Gram was my cat's name in California."

"The one that was my mom's guardian? Wow!" Studying a rock, Emma sticks it in one of her pockets and walks towards us. "Was he a magic cat like Spike?"

"He was pretty cool, so I think he probably had some magic cat powers." Moving warily, I bend down to see how cold the water is.

Too cold for this girl.

Okay. Enough. It's time to get back on the bike and see what the rest of this world looks like. I don't know exactly what happened. I have my suspicions, but my first priority is to make sure that Emma is safe.

Old stories passed down, letters tucked away for years, dreams, even memories that resurface feel different when you experience them. For now, I need to keep my personal reactions tucked away.

Wow. That word is on an automatic scroll through my thoughts. Wow. Wow. Wow.

I take a long look at the lake and the trees and hills around us, as I try to reconcile this landscape with the one that had been here fifteen minutes ago.

"Em, let's go back to the Fiddlehead and check things out."

Watchful and deliberate, I walk back across the wet rocks to Emma. Spike scampers close behind. My clothes are damp from the spray of the waves, and I feel sandy. I pick Spike up and automatically scratch under his chin.

"Let's dry off Spike's paws and get going."

Arms wrapped around Emma and Spike, I squeeze them as I nuzzle Emma's head. Spike squeaks in protest, and I loosen my grip as Emma giggles. We hold hands and hike up the hill past the fountain to my bike. I have to run my free hand across the stones as we pass.

It's real.

I breathe a deep sigh of relief when I see my bike. I don't know how this works. The landscape is altered. What if my bike had changed too? As I look around, I'm reminded that this is not the same place we rode up to. I don't know anywhere in North Dakota like this. It's Washington State and British Columbia green. Not North Dakota green.

Emma's no longer holding onto my hand. I turn around from my examination of the Trumpet to see her staring up at the trees.

"Is this magic? Is this even real?" Spike leaps out of her grasp. With the clothesline trailing behind him, he jumps on the bike. Dazed, Emma slowly walks over and leans her head against me.

CHAPTER 7

I wrap my arms around her and squeeze her. "Of course this is real. I don't know if it's magic, but you and Spike and I are here, and we're real. We'll figure this out, Em. I promise." She continues staring at the trees.

"Let's get Spike dried off and tucked away before we get ready." I let go of her and step over and pick him up. Spike's purrs reach maximum sound levels as we dry him off.

"Spike sounds almost as loud as the Trumpet." Emma grins as she settles him into the saddlebag.

In no time at all, we're zipped up, sunnies and gauntlets on, helmets fastened, and Emma is settled behind me.

Please start.

Turning the key, I hear the familiar soft growl of my bike. I exhale and shift into first.

Thank you. I honestly didn't know if the Trumpet would start. I'm so freakin' scared right now. All of my years of learning how to stay calm and cool have disintegrated. This is not a situation I can control, but how do I maintain my composure? Oh, yeah, right. Take care of business, Sellis. Just breathe.

Emma squeezes my waist. "Let's roll, Gram."

And so that's what we do.

There are changes everywhere. The barely-there path we followed to the fountain is now a gravel road that's being used. We ride past combines, swathers, and grain trucks left overnight and ready to go. No movement yet, but people will be showing up soon to start their day.

So much has happened and changed for us, and the day has barely begun.

Flocks of Canada geese fill the sky and cover the fields. There are hundreds, maybe even thousands, of them. Their honking surrounds us. Mixed in are flocks of blackbirds and other birds I can't identify. The autumn migration is in full swing here.

To be honest, I will be more comfortable once we reach the Fiddlehead and see how it's changed. At least there I have a framework. Out here, I know nothing.

Hiding behind those thoughts are the whispers. *You're crazy. This isn't real. Snap out of it before you hurt Emma or yourself. Like mother, like daughter.*

I speed up and scan the road and trees and fields. As I drive, I fall into automatic riding mode, which helps ease my mind.

Emma's hands are loosely draped on my waist. I feel her humming, which is what she does when she's nervous or uncomfortable. I take some comfort in the fact that she doesn't have an iron grip on me. She trusts me. I need to be relaxed and strong for her. I don't want her freaking out because I am.

Calm down, Sellis. Like your father-in-law used to say, keep the bike between the weeds. Oh my God, I've become a cliché on wheels.

And right then, I see the sign.

"Welcome to Crystal Springs. Friendly people, good food, and the best damn water in the world."

What the heck? This hadn't been here when we left. It's not the typical green and white sign that line the roads at home, but it's in English, which is good.

Huh. The water I know about. Now let's see about the friendly people.

Everything seems somewhat familiar, only expanded and enlarged, if that makes any sense. More trees and grass. Even the color of the sky is a deeper shade of blue. Did it take us this long to drive to the fountain?

Is time different here? Nah. The time thing I will attribute to nerves.

I see buildings and moving vehicles ahead. A maroon pickup goes past, and the driver nods his head and raises his right index finger off the steering wheel in the classic Midwestern wave. Not only are there people here, but based on that simple greeting, I know they're my kind of people.

We drive past the intact brick schoolhouse, along with other buildings and houses. I can't believe all the trees here.

Emma's song stops abruptly. I know she's noticed the town. Her body stiffens, and both hands are now wrapped around my waist.

Up ahead, there's another sign beside the road. Beyond it is a white house.

"Fiddlehead Fern Bed & Breakfast - Daily, Weekly, and Monthly Rates Available."

The sign is a work of art. Written in calligraphy in

blues, yellows and reds, the words are wrapped in vibrant green leaves and vines. It looks like a piece of the grounds was put up on the sign. The house seems larger, and feathery plumes of ferns surround the foundation and fill the yard. Tall, stately trees form a canopy around the lawn.

We turn into the driveway, and I pull up to the garage door. Before I turn off the bike, my mind runs through different scenarios and explanations. I'm nervous. No. I'm afraid.

The cacophony of the geese and other birds is more noticeable without the low rumble of my bike. Emma immediately hops off and starts talking as she paces back and forth.

"Gram, what is going on? Where did this town come from? How did it grow? Did we really time travel? Could we be in a coma?"

"Em, breathe! We're at the Fiddlehead in Crystal Springs, and we'll get answers in a minute. Take off your helmet and gloves and let Spike out," I reply as I get off the bike and undo the strap of my helmet. Despite my anxiety, I laugh to myself at Emma's questions, because I'm wondering the exact same things.

Barking erupts from inside the house. Next thing I know, a blur of fur comes flying around the corner. A small, furry, brown tornado and a huge, yellow one bound toward us.

Maybe Spike should stay in his bag a while longer.

"Em, stay here by the bike for a sec, okay? Hey, buddies. What's up?" I walk over to the dogs, making small talk as I take off my gloves. Their barking isn't aggressive; it's questioning and welcoming. "Where are your people?

Are they coming? We're friendly. Are you?" As I bend down to let the Pekinese with the frantically swishing tail sniff my hand, I get a wet lick across my nose from the Labrador.

Standing up, I hear Emma giggle. I turn and see Spike on her back as she tries to stand up. Spike's tail is straight up, and he's fluffed up at least twice his normal size.

"Gram, he's purring and fluffing at the same time." Pulling Spike around to her chest, she straightens up and looks at me.

No longer barking, but with tails wagging in overtime, both dogs look expectantly at me as though they're saying, "Hey there, strangers. What's happening?"

They wag their way over to Emma and Spike, and I follow. Back at the bike, I take off my jacket and put it on the seat as I hear a voice coming our way.

"Em, come over here, and let me help you."

"Leo. Sheba. I know. I know. Someone is here."

The dogs run to greet the woman, barking updates about the newcomers. She laughs as she tousles the labrador's head and looks at us and smiles. I glance at Emma and Spike, just as Spike leaps down and sashays over to the dogs and woman.

"Spike, come back here." Emma is right behind him.

She looks like me. (No extra limbs or eyes that I can see from here.) Maybe a little younger than I am. She's in jeans and a t-shirt, too. There's a dishtowel draped over one shoulder and her chestnut colored hair is pulled back in a messy bun. She pulls a pair of glasses off the top of her head and puts them on as she walks over to me.

I smile in return as I walk over to join in the melee.

"Hello! My name is Sellis, and this is my granddaughter, Emma, and our cat, Spike. We're wondering if you have a room available?"

"As a matter of fact, we do," she says as she reaches out her hand to shake mine. "Welcome to the Fiddlehead. My name is Grace. Are you planning to stay awhile or only tonight?"

"I'm not sure," I reply, "I better find out first if you allow cats."

"Well, if your cat can put up with these two, he's welcome. We also have cats, but they're either sleeping or patrolling," Grace says as she bends to pet Spike, who is now doing figure eights around her legs.

Emma is sitting cross-legged on the ground with the Pekinese on her lap, while the Labrador alternates sniffs and kisses on her. After sending a brief prayer of thanks to the Universe, I begin to learn about this version of Crystal Springs.

CHAPTER 8

Spike jumps onto Emma's shoulder and drapes himself around her neck. Settled into his usual spot, he reaches down and bats at the Pekinese. The Labrador walks behind Emma and is sniffing her hair as Spike's tail flips across his face. Giggles, purrs, and yips of canine pleasure provide a reassuring background to my conversation.

The house has been in Grace's family for generations, and it was transformed into a bed and breakfast a few years ago. She owns it with her partner, Anne, who is running errands and should be back any time.

"I'm a classic case. I couldn't wait to grow up and see the world. It turns out that a part of me was always back here. My grandpa died a few years ago, and my family didn't know what to do with this house. I came back for his funeral. One thing led to another, and here I am. An unplanned career as an innkeeper, a new love, all back in my hometown. Go figure." Grace makes a sweeping motion with her dishtowel.

Grace's open manner reassures me and something about her makes me feel at ease. "Anne and I both grew up here, and our families have been part of the Springs since the beginning. We both went away to school and now here we are. Are you from around here? It looks like you two girls are on a road trip."

I've been worried about how to broach the subject of "where" we are. She makes me feel comfortable enough to come right out and ask.

"This might sound strange. I'm not quite sure we're where we…"

Grace finishes my sentence; "Where you started from?"

"Exactly!" My shoulders relax. "We left Crystal Springs earlier this morning to look at the fountain, and, oh, I don't know how to say this. This is Crystal Springs, North Dakota, right?"

"The fountain!" Another voice joins Grace. I'm surprised to see someone, because I didn't hear any vehicles. The lab dashes down the driveway to greet the woman that I assume is Anne. She's in jeans and tennies, with her blond hair pulled back in a braid. Aviator sunnies cover her eyes. She's wearing a back pack and there's another canvas bag draped over one shoulder. They're laughing as they repeat "the fountain."

"Leo, get down. There's nothing in here for you." Anne looks questioningly at Emma, Spike and me, and then at Grace.

"Anne, meet Sellis, Emma, and Spike. They visited the fountain this morning."

Grace then reassures me that we're in Crystal Springs and it is 2018. I'm right though. It isn't the same Crystal Springs we left earlier this morning. Emma and I traveled from our world to theirs through the fountain, which is, in fact, a portal. But, she adds, not all the time, or for everyone.

Right now, I feel like I've stepped into a fantasy book. Concepts that I've read about over the years exist. We've passed through a portal into an alternative universe. A parallel world. We found a portal. A portal. Oh. My. God.

As Grace talks, my attention wanders. How am I going to contact Caleb? How do we get home? Can we get back? Will we ever be able to return to Willow Banks?

I force myself to concentrate as Grace continues, "The fountain's known as a portal. How and why it works, I can't say. To me, it feels like magic, although I've also heard scientific explanations for it. It involves the spring, and the water flow. The fountain itself isn't that old in your world. It's been here in one form or another for generations. In fact, one of my ancestors built the original."

Grace takes my hand, "I know you're feeling overwhelmed. I promise that you, Emma, and Spike are safe. We'll do our best to answer your questions."

"I agree. We've got a lot to talk about. But, first I really want to take a closer look at your bike. Is that a Triumph?" Anne slides the backpack off and sets it down beside her bag. "Leo, leave it, not yours." It turns out that they both ride motorcycles. In fact, they don't even own a car.

At my look of surprise, Anne tells me, "We have all kinds of bikes and scooters, and bicycles here. They're a more popular common form of transportation because they're economical and fuel efficient. There are trucks and farm machinery here, too, as you've seen. And of course, cars. We just believe in a slower way of life. We discovered that many of the modern conveniences, so to speak, take away something from savoring the simple pleasures."

Anne pauses when Grace reaches over and squeezes her shoulder. She takes a deep breath.

"I'm sorry. I'm preaching. I've been in your world, and I appreciate your way of life. I simply value and prefer our world. I know you have a million questions, and you're both probably starving. Let's go inside. We'll show you your room. Once you unpack and clean up, we'll eat and talk."

Grace adds, "Anne is one of the best advocates of our way of life. She's a professor in our university system and a librarian. I'm excited to hear your story, too."

"Great." I glance over at Emma as they head back into the house, "Let's be careful around Em. I'm not sure how she'll react. She's an old soul in so many ways, and sometimes it's easy to forget she's only nine."

Out of the corner of my eye, I notice something in the trees beyond the garage. Heading around the corner, I softly call, "Tawny."

A rustle of branches and she swoops over my head and lands on the garage roof. Gazing down, she gives a long, low hoot.

Looking over at me, Emma says, "Gram, Tawny is scolding you. She must think we tried to ditch her."

I look up at Tawny, and can't help grinning because she found us again.

"Hello to you too, Tawny! Too bad we don't have a snack like a frozen mouse for her, huh, Em? Maybe I should start keeping a stash of them in my bag next to your gum?"

"Yuck. Gram, you are so gross," Emma gags as I start to unpack the bike.

Tawny flies back to the trees as we enter the house.

CHAPTER 9

This house is huge! Is everything here bigger? Ha. It has two stories like the other B&B, but it's a different style, with a wrap-around porch. I wish I knew more about architecture. Lily would know. I just know what I like. Like this big old porch. And the feathery plumes of the inn's namesake ferns that I see everywhere. I need to grow more ferns at home.

Her head tilted back to take it all in, Emma informs me, "I'm going to name this house the Elegant Galleon. It looks like one of those sailing ships you see in bottles."

We walk right into the kitchen, where Grace stands at the sink. "Just head up the stairs and down the hall." She motions with a large beet. *I think everything IS bigger.* "I'll have sandwiches ready in a bit, okay?"

Another cozy bedroom filled with sunshine welcomes us. A miniature jungle of plants cascades and vines around the room. I hear the rustling of poplar trees through the open windows, and I picture my wind trees at home. That sound reminds me that we're a very long way from home, and I am not in control of this situation. Which is not where I like to be.

Breathe. Everything will be all right.

Emma and Spike check out the four-poster bed we get to share.

"No kicking allowed, Emma. And I don't want to wake up with your foot in my ear, okay?" I look at her reflection in the mirror in the attached bathroom. The cold water revives me as I wipe off the road dust from my face and get myself under control.

"What? Me, kick you? Never, right, Spike?" Giggling, she gets off the bed. "Come on, Gram, let's go eat. I'm starving."

After lunch, while Grace and Anne clean up, Emma and I go out to the porch. The furniture beckons me to sit down and relax. Similar to our room upstairs, there is a veritable jungle here, too, with many of the same old fashioned plants I have at home. A variegated spider plant with cascades of babies sways in the breeze, along with a gigantic Boston fern and a glossy Swedish ivy. Dozens of pots filled with colorful flowers line the railing.

Sprawled on the floor, Emma is covered by fur. Spike's black and white tuxedo markings contrast with the brown and yellow shades of the two dogs. They've become best friends, and Emma is the leader of the pack. Looking at them, I can't help but smile. She's singing, and it feels like home.

I pick up a book from the table next to the wicker rocker where I sit. It's the Crystal Springs Centennial book for the years 1887 to 1987. How funny, it looks just like the one from my hometown.

Now that I'm sitting still, my thoughts start whirling again.

It does feel like home. I mean, normal. How can that be? How can this be? I know, I wondered if something like this was possible. But to actually be here... In another world? Breathe. Listen. Ask questions. There's a reason you're here.

Grace and Anne join us. I have to ask about their house.

"How old is this house? It's beautiful."

"Thank you. It was built about 1890," Grace says as she lifts a large, orange tabby off the chair next to me. "Our families came from Boston and Concord and the New England region. They incorporated their Cape Cod-style into the classic Prairie, and Craftsman-style homes often found here. When you walk around town, you'll see other houses like ours."

As she tells it, the town was first settled in the 1860s. Many of the early residents moved from the East Coast. Some of them were part of a naturalist and environmental movement, which originated with Thoreau. Over time, more family members followed, along with like-minded settlers and immigrants from Europe.

"Okay, I have to be honest. We're sitting here talking about your hometown and your ancestors. Just having a regular conversation. But at the same time, I can't stop wondering if this is really happening." My voice is shaky. When I see Emma turn to look at me, I stop and take a breath.

"I get it, Sellis. We're as real as you and Emma. People show up here for a variety of reasons. Some deliberately come because they know they have family ties, others show up because of a gut feeling." Anne leans over from the couch beside me and points at the book. "We have a written history of all the 'beginning families,' as we call them, and we have scribes who keep as current as they can, scattered between both worlds. "

My fingers tap-dance across the book in my lap. *Yes! Families! Grandma Flossie!*

"It's interesting that you mention family history. That's part of why we're here. I think I had family here decades ago. My mom told me stories about visiting her grandmother in Crystal Springs, but there's nothing left in the other Crystal Springs."

Grace grins, "You've come to the right spot. Anne is in the middle of updating our family history, along with the town history."

"What was your grandma's name? Do you know anything about her background? Hang on a sec. I've got some more books in my office." Anne is up and asking questions as she goes back into the house.

Grace watches her, then turns to me. Shrugging her shoulders, she smiles, "And just like that, there she goes. That's Anne. She loves a mystery."

My attention returns to our immediate situation.

"How does this all work? Is there a time difference between the worlds? How about dates and years? How, or why is the climate different?"

My barrage of questions comes to a stop when the cat in Anne's lap jumps down and walks over. With a smile, I pick him up and continue.

"You said that sometimes the portal doesn't work, why is that? And why doesn't it work for everyone? Can't anyone pass through it?"

Emma sits up. "Can campers go through? Maybe next time we can bring the dogs and Mom and Gramps along."

"How many portals are there? Can we ever go home? Can we communicate with my husband and daughter?" I continue stroking the cat to keep calm.

Grace replies, "Because we're the only ones who can use the portals anymore, I suspect we'll discover that you're descended from one of the original families. Non-family members or vehicles can travel with us. That's what we call it when you use a portal: traveling. Which is why you're called travelers."

"I can accept that part of this journey. Now, talk to me about cell phones and technology. If my cell phone doesn't work, how do I contact Caleb?" I ask as I picture my phone tucked away in my backpack. "He's going to become frantic if he doesn't hear from me soon. I'm sorry that I'm babbling. I just have so many questions!"

"We have cell phones, and yes, even Internet access. You can't call Caleb from here, though, because cell phones don't work between our worlds. There's a concept those providers would love, right? As a community, we decided to limit our personal online use, although it is available," Grace explains. "Libraries, hospitals, and schools have access. Private homes and small businesses usually choose not to, though, because the cost would be prohibitive."

"I know you were shocked that we don't own a car." I nod when Grace looks at me. "If we're going long dis-tances, of course, we'll use a car or SUV, but we also make use of biofuels. There are a few plants now in the state and south of us where it's not as hilly, you'll find wind turbines. We utilize geothermal energy in most of our schools and businesses."

"Hey, Sellis, what's your grandma's full name?" Anne

comes back with an armful of books and papers. "Sorry to interrupt you, Grace. Although it's probably a good thing. I don't want Sellis to run off because you're preaching."

"Florence Sellis Weaver. And I love what I'm hearing from Grace, so no worries."

"Look up her name in the Centennial book you're holding, would you please?"

Sitting down on the floor, she puts the pile next to her. Emma walks on her knees over to her.

"What did you find?" she says as she picks up a book. Spike saunters over to assist, a faint rumble of purrs emanating from him.

"Oh, my gosh." I see Florence Weaver's name listed in the index. Turning to page 347, I find a brief history of her.

At the same time, Emma holds up a book and blurts out, "Hey, she's got an owl, just like you."

"What? An owl?" Grace goes over to see.

"I knew you were related to one of the original families," Anne declares. "There was no way you would've gotten here if you weren't. And, Sellis, I also think we're related. Distantly, but related, nonetheless. Welcome home, cousin!"

Caleb and I had discussed the possibility that there was another Crystal Springs. Granted, there were times the discussions involved late nights and bottles of wine. I hadn't wholly believed we would or could find our way here. To be standing in another world is a more significant leap of faith than I've ever experienced. Discovering Grandma Flossie lived in this town, and that I could have other family, feels surreal.

"I'm going to go over to the school." Anne stands up with a preoccupied look on her face. She's got a sheaf of papers in one hand. "I'm pretty sure I can find some more information about your family there. If you like, you two could walk to our library and talk to Seth. He's the librarian. I'll stop by and let him know you're coming."

I agree. A walk will help me gather my thoughts. Grace gives me directions. "The dogs and Spike can go, too. The dogs know the way, so don't worry about getting lost. Seth knows them pretty well."

Emma is on her way upstairs to get Spike's leash before Grace is done talking.

Picking up the book Emma had laid down, I shake my head when I see the picture of my grandma Flossie standing next to an owl on a fence post.

"What are the chances? It says that she was known for gardening and her abilities to work with and heal animals of all kinds."

"I take it you also have a green thumb? I already know you're an animal lover." Chuckling, Grace bends down and picks Spike up off the book pile.

"I do. I have a greenhouse and nursery business back home with my husband, Caleb, and daughter, Lily. I wish our climate was more like yours. I wonder why they're so different. Ours has changed some, but it feels more like the northwest part of the country here. I bet you don't get snow, do you?"

"Nope. No snow, but we do get rains. And they're due any day." Grace continues petting Spike as she tells me she's heard stories about certain animals having the ability to go between worlds without using portals. That would explain how Tawny has been able to follow us.

Hmmm. I wonder if I could get Tawny to go back to Caleb, so he knows we're safe.

I started researching falconry because of my bond with Tawny. One day, I halfway seriously asked Caleb if he thought she could deliver messages. We made leather anklets and jesses, which are thin leather straps attached to them, for her. I can't fasten messages, but by switching the jesses, Caleb and I have created a simple communication system.

This could be a win, win situation. If Tawny can return to Caleb, the theory about select animals being able to travel between our worlds is proven. Plus, Caleb would know we're okay.

Spike's leash is on, and the pack is ready.

"Em, let's find Tawny. Then we'll go check out the library."

Outside, I call Tawny's name as I walk over to my bike to get my bird bag. Emma, Spike, and the two dogs, Sheba, the Pekinese, and Leo, the Labrador, follow close behind.

Watching Emma play with the beasts, I wonder if I did the right thing by bringing her along. I never thought any harm would come to us. I've been riding motorcycles for years, so I wasn't nervous about that. The magical part of the discovery of the portal wasn't totally unexpected, but it adds an unknown element. If it were only me, I would be fine.

Emma seems to be her inquisitive, lively self. We'd

talked about the trip and the possibility that there might be unexpected events.

Did I believe it would happen? In my heart, I hoped so. Of course, speculating and wondering is a lot different than reality. This isn't the first time I've had brushes with unexplainable events, so I was open to anything.

Now that we're here, I hope and pray getting home is as simple as returning to the fountain. Poof. We'll turn the water on and soon be back in our world.

A swoosh makes me pause and look up as Tawny flies overhead.

"Tawny, hello, sweet pea!" I raise my hand in the sign I devised to let her know I need to touch her jesses. Putting on my heavy falconry glove, I hold out my right arm. She flies to the Trumpet and lands on my arm.

"Hoot," Emma runs over. "Hoot to you, Tawny."

I lower her down onto the bike seat.

Stroking her head, I say, "Emma, grab one of the jesses from my bird bag, please."

I undo the clasp on Tawny's right ankle and remove the dark-brown jess and replace it with a tan one. Her piercing yellow eyes follow my every move as I do her left one.

"Go home to Caleb, Tawny. Be safe, owlet, and please come back to me." I stroke the top of her head once more before stepping back. She hoots and then flies away. We watch her for a few minutes until she disappears.

CHAPTER 10

Grace is chopping vegetables when I walk back into the kitchen.

"How late is the library open?" I snatch a piece of broccoli from the growing pile.

She glances up at the round, mint-green metal clock over the sink.

"Um, it's a little after three. Because it's Tuesday, it'll be open till 5:30. You'll have plenty of time. It'll take about ten, fifteen minutes to get there depending on how fast you walk.

"Tell Seth hello, he's a good friend of ours. Now that I think about it, he's probably another cousin. Anne was going to stop in and let him know you're coming. Who knows what kind of information he'll dig up for you. Oh, hey, he's done a lot of traveling himself, too."

"Thanks, Grace. See you in a bit." Backpack slung over my shoulder, I join Emma and Spike and the dogs on the porch. The dogs take off down the steps with Emma following close behind.

Spike strolls along, his clothes-line leash dragging behind. I catch up with him and pick up his leash. It droops loosely from my hand as he saunters beside me, his tail curved into a question mark. Emma skips between the dogs, and I watch as she bends down to ruffle Sheba's ears and pat Leo's head as he leans into her as they walk.

There are no sidewalks at first, so we stay along the side of the road. That soon changes and the houses increase. Many of them are large beauties like the Fiddlehead, with ample lots filled with oaks, elms, towering cottonwood trees, and flowers. Oh, my. There are flowers everywhere.

It's an established neighborhood from a different era. Picturesque, traditional farmhouses stand next to Victorian homes with beveled leaded glass windows gleaming in the afternoon sun.

And porches. These porches are well used and lived on. They're filled with toys and sweatshirts draped over railings, shoes, and sandals discarded among the rocking chairs and swings. Flower pots are perched upon and hanging from every available space.

There must have been a covenant in the city building codes requiring porches.

People are doing yard work. Several of them glance up and wave. Just like back home, kids are riding bikes and playing. Dogs bark or run out to greet us as we go by.

As I walk, I marvel at the normalcy surrounding me while I'm in the middle of a surreal experience.

"There it is, Gram. It's that big, yellow house." With a burst of speed, Emma and the dogs take off.

By the time Spike and I arrive, they're through the front door. I guess animals are allowed anywhere in this town. We definitely are not in Kansas anymore. Or, for that matter, at home in Willow Banks.

There's a sign similar to the one at the Fiddlehead in the front yard. We're at the City of Crystal Springs Literary Society. I love the lettering and embellishments and stop and pull out my phone so I can take a picture. Oh, right. My phone doesn't work here. I'll have to bring my camera when I return.

The front door opens as we walk up the sidewalk. Emma smiles as she extends her arm to guide us in.

I step into a large room lined with shelves. Books of all sizes and colors, a veritable smorgasbord, with no discernible rhyme or reason, overflows them. The sun glows through tall windows. To my left, an oversized, maroon velvet couch that says, "hello, come plop on me" is centered behind a low wooden coffee table piled with more books and magazines.

The dogs are standing in front of a counter to my right. Their tails swish madly back and forth as they look up at the man leaning over it, talking to them.

"Ta-Da! Here they are!" Emma announces. The man looks up and smiles as he walks around the counter. Sun-bleached brown hair is pulled back into a ponytail, and deep brown eyes twinkle as he extends his hand. He's dressed in blue jeans and sneakers with the sleeves of his blue and white striped shirt rolled up.

"Hi, Gram and Spike. Welcome to the library. I'm Seth. I'm very pleased to meet you and Emma. Anne stopped by and told me you were on the way."

"Grace says hello, too. She would've come with, but she's cooking."

"Lucky you. I wonder what culinary delight she's got in store for you. Anytime I can wrangle an invite to eat with them, I'm there. So. You two ladies are travelers. I've done my share of traveling, but it's been a while. Were you ready for it, or was it a surprise?"

"Even though I thought it might happen, it was a surprise. I don't know if you can ever prepare yourself for something like this," I hold out my arms to encompass the room and Seth nods. "How do you explain this to someone?"

We both laugh as Seth says, "I understand!"

Emma goes to find a book to read while I tell Seth about my search for Grandma Flossie. I'm giddy and exhilarated about the pictures and information I found with Grace and Anne.

"Those are great sources and good places for me to start. I've got the same books here. Let's see what else I can find." Picking up a pencil and paper, we head to the local history section. As we walk, he's writing and talking and grabbing books.

I'm soon settled at a table with a pile of books. The stack in front of me is an assortment of sizes and content, varying from dry, factual listings of property and businesses to high school annuals and family histories.

Leo and Sheba are under my table, keeping watch. Or maybe they're sleeping. I hear sounds like snoring.

Emma is lying on the couch with a book. Spike is on her stomach, curled up in his favorite sleeping position.

Grandma Flossie's name pops out at me from a binder filled with newsletters. They remind me of the weekly newspaper I grew up reading. The current events include visits the locals received from friends and family.

Florence Sellis Weaver.

I almost fall off my chair. *Oh my gosh.*

She had family visiting from Iowa. The weather was typically warm. They enjoyed her beautiful flower and vegetable gardens and orchards.

Not only do I have her name, but I've also inherited her green thumb. I think fondly of my greenhouses and the business I've "grown" from my knowledge and love of plants and herbs.

All right. I've established Grandma Flossie lived here. Maybe she came from Iowa? I'll have to reread her letters. I wonder if there are any return addresses or other clues on them.

When Seth comes in with another book for me, I share my discovery. He jots down the Iowa information, and as he writes, I notice a tattoo of a book and a compass on his forearm entwined by a heart. I show him the paw print surrounded by a heart with ivy leaves on my left wrist.

"They're my guild signs," he explains. "I have my Master's in Library Science, and I worked on that while I was traveling. Tattoos have been a tradition here with a long history. Most adults have at least one tattoo that will tell you what their passion is or their craft. It's interesting, without even knowing our history, you've done that, too."

Tracing the heart of my tattoo reminds me that I needed this particular tattoo to honor the animals I've loved and shared my life with. The heart surrounding the paw print was a given, while the addition of the ivy leaves was a natural addition.

There's no such thing as coincidence. This is just another knock from the Universe on my conventional, ordinary door.

Time to regroup and figure out my next steps. I've established that Florence Sellis Weaver lived here. Mom told us she was her grandmother, so I knew her as Great Grandma Flossie. Yet, we never met any other relatives of Mom's. Why? I've spent my life being compliant and not questioning my mom's secrets, but I'm not going to do that any longer.

Hold on tightly, Emma. I think our ride is just beginning.

I pile up the books to take back to Seth and put my notebook and pens in my backpack. Pushing back my chair, I stand up and stretch. My movements disrupt the dogs, and I watch them wake up.

"Are you guys ready to move? Go get Emma and Spike so we can go home." I bend down and pat Sheba on the head as she strolls past, and feel Leo's tail swish against my legs when he goes by.

Standing at the counter I shake my head. "I still cannot believe Grandma Flossie lived here. There's almost nothing left of Crystal Springs where I live. To be honest, I wasn't sure I'd find anything about her."

Sliding the books over, Seth taps his fingers on them.

"Having something tangible to start with makes a world of difference, doesn't it? There are going to be more records. I'm going to look at land records and more Springs history archives. The city has meticulous records; it's just a matter of finding the right places."

He keeps talking as he sorts the books.

"Between my library resources and Anne's, we'll find answers. Grace and Anne both come from the founding families. Anne's family even has their own library."

Turning away, he picks up a couple of books.

"I have a couple of books for you to look through. This one is a history of the Springs and the founding families, the other one is more philosophical. It describes who we are as a people. I think you'll find them both helpful."

Glancing over at Emma, he continues, "Emma's in the middle of a book and, at the rate she's reading, it looks like she'll finish it in a couple of hours. If you don't have a chance to bring it back, Anne or Grace will get it back to me."

A ping from his computer makes him turn away.

"I entered your mom's name into the computer to do a search of the archives. Maybe I got a hit. I didn't know if I'd hear back today since it's close to five."

"Seth, this is extremely weird. You and Grace and Anne are so nonchalant about our worlds. I think I'm operating on autopilot while trying to be composed about all this."

Fumbling with my backpack, I set it on the counter to add the books.

"Sellis, I know what a big deal this is. It's more common to see travelers here than in your world, but trust me, none of us take it for granted," Seth responds as he looks me in the eyes and reaches out and squeezes my hand.

His comments make me feel better, and I manage to get the books into my backpack. Amid a flurry of wagging tails and thank you's and see you soon's, we head out. Emma and the dogs run to the sidewalk while Spike and I follow.

"Sellis! You're not going to believe what I've got." I stop and turn around to see Seth waving papers at me.

Taking a step towards him, I turn to see where Emma and the dogs are. They're about a half a block away.

"Emma, come back. We need to look at something."

Seth grins and shakes his head as he meets me halfway.

"It looks like your mom didn't only visit here, Sellis. She lived here." He hands me a sheet of paper.

Glancing down, I see a newspaper story and a picture. My mom's name leaps out at me: Sophie Weaver, Crystal Springs Valedictorian for the class of 1955. My hands are shaking; my eyes get blurry.

"Gram, what's wrong? Why are you crying?" Panting, Emma wraps her arms around me. Leo and Sheba start barking as they circle around us.

"Emma, I'm okay. Seth found something amazing, and it took me by surprise." I hold the paper out so Emma can see, and lean my head on hers.

"All of a sudden, papers started coming out of the fax machine. These are only the first pages from the archive search of your mom's name." Seth fans out the sheaf of papers. "Here, take these, too."

After everything else that's happened today, I'm having trouble processing this.

In some ways, it feels like another lifetime instead of one day. The fact that I'm standing in an alternative universe doesn't faze me. The realization that my mom had been here, though... affects me.

"I've got to close the library. I'll bring the rest of the pages by later tonight. And who knows, maybe there'll be leftovers. Or pie."

He winks at Emma and holds up his hand for a fist bump.

"No wonder you're such a smart gal, Em. It runs in the family."

"What's a valedictorian, Gram? Are you one? Can I be one?" Emma asks as she fist bumps Seth.

Giving my shoulder a quick squeeze, Seth goes back to the library. Emma hands me the sheet of paper and whirls around, "Okay, Gram, we'll meet you." Off she goes with the dogs close behind.

"Well, Spike, it looks like it's you and me, buddy." There's no acknowledgement from him, he's engrossed in grooming himself. Stooping down, I pick him up and walk back to the road again, as I sort through my thoughts.

The sound of honking geese cuts through the haze of my thoughts, and I stop and look as they fly overhead. Their honking drowns out the neighborhood sounds of bird songs, barking dogs, and kids playing. Watching them recede brings me back to the here and now.

I think of Tawny. Is she safe? That makes me think of Caleb. I know he's going to be concerned he hasn't heard from me by now.

I walk up the driveway as Emma and the dogs go round the corner of the house. The practical side of me kicks in as I walk past my bike. I need to find a place to park it overnight.

Priority is one-on-one time with Emma to make sure she's doing all right. Then I need to sit down with Grace and Anne. I have a million more questions. Going through my mental checklist, I keep returning to the thought that Mom lived here. My mom lived in this town. I'm a grandma for heavens sake, and this is the first personal bit of information I've ever had about my own mother.

It's cool and exciting. But also sad.

The screen door slams and I hear, "Grandma, we're having homemade peach ice cream for supper."

Well. It doesn't get much better than that.

CHAPTER 11

Before supper, and in our room, I brush Emma's hair so I can re-braid it. This is a ritual that began back with her mom and I carry it on with Emma. It's also one of my favorite relaxation techniques.

"Your hair is just like your mom's, thick and wavy. It's got a lot of copper highlights in it now from being outside so much this summer."

Emma takes a chunk of her hair and holds it up to look.

"I remember when I taught myself how to French braid by practicing on your mom. She even had me braid her friend's hair when they came over. I think that's why I love doing this so much." The memories of giggling pre-teen girls trying their best to sit still as I brush and braid their hair make me smile. I love that I've created a small tradition with my family.

Spike sprawls across Emma's lap and stares up at her, the look he usually gives when he wants serious petting.

"Gram, have you ever talked to anyone else who has gone to another world like us?"

Boom! That's my girl. I didn't even have to initiate the subject.

"Nope. I've only read books about it."

"Yeah. Me, too. That's why it's kinda hard to believe it's happening. Because this is real. How can that be?" She turns her head to look at me with her brow furrowed in concentration. It's the same expression that I've seen countless times before on her mother. Man, genetics never fails to astonish me. Letting go of the braid, I wrap my arms around Emma, pulling her close.

"Are you scared?"

"No. You're here, and you always take care of me. I know it's really happening. This isn't like a movie set or something."

I squeeze her tight before I let her go. "This would be quite the movie location, huh, wouldn't it? Almost as good as Jurassic Park, right?"

She's fine.

I leave it at that and finish her braid as we move on to more important topics. Like wondering if Spike and Tawny talk to each other, or if they're even friends, and how cool it would be if we could talk to them, and finally, the pros and cons of dark nail polish colors versus light.

"I am so full I could burst." Emma groans as she slides down in her chair. "That was the best food I've ever eaten, except for Gram's and my mom's. Since they don't make homemade ice cream, it might be the best food ever."

The 'best food ever' consisted of minestrone soup, whole grain bread, and peach ice cream. All homemade.

Along with mead for the big girls. It was brewed at a monastery in western North Dakota. I tuck away the thought of learning to make my own mead at home.

"Mom didn't talk about herself or any family other than Grandma Flossie," I say. "We never met anyone else, just her."

Then it hits me. I have been here, to this Crystal Springs. Mom brought us here. This is where we would go when she'd take off with us. No wonder Dad couldn't find us. That's why I had that inexplicable sense of familiarity when we walked to the library. Although the town has grown and changed over the years, and I was a kid, I remember it.

"Do you know why your mom didn't talk about her family? Do you have family on your dad's side?" Grace asks. "I'm sorry. Am I being intrusive? I know we just met, yet I feel so comfortable with you two."

"North Dakota Nice." Anne and I say together, and the three of us start laughing.

"What does that mean? Why are you guys laughing?" Emma looks at each of us as though we're aliens.

"It's a phrase used to describe the easy and comfortable way some people get along with each other," I say.

"Especially when you meet, and you feel like you've known each other for a long time," Anne adds.

"Oh, okay," Emma shrugs.

"I think my parents isolated us because of Mom's mental illness."

"It was out of bounds, and we never talked about it when I was growing up. In fact, my dad always denied that there was anything wrong with Mom, to his dying day. That old saying about kids being seen and not heard was law in my house. No questions or comments. Ever."

I stop and look down at my hands. They're clenched so tight, I feel my nails digging into my palms. *Sellis. Just breathe.* I open them and rub them on my jeans. Take a deep breath and continue.

"I never knew anything about her family or background either. As a result, I grew up being evasive and avoiding certain topics. Even my little sis, Kate, and I didn't talk about the things that happened to us when we were kids. There were some traumatic times, and we got good at blocking them off. In retrospect, who knows what my mom blocked out, or ran away from. Learning that she lived here is a major discovery for me."

Grace stands up and says, "Thank you for sharing, Sellis. Mental illness is still hard to talk about today, isn't it?" She squeezes my shoulder and begins to gather dishes.

"I'm going to get the kitchen cleaned up, and then I think we should have a fire and enjoy this summer evening," she continues. "Knowing Seth, he'll be here soon."

"Emma, I'm going to feed the dogs, do you want to help?" The words aren't even out of Anne's mouth before the dogs start barking.

A golden glow infuses the backyard. The sun hasn't set, and it's still warm enough, so we don't need jackets. It's a perfect late summer night.

The dogs announce Seth's arrival. He walks up with a bulging envelope folder.

"Hello, ladies. I come bearing news." The dogs sniff him as he walks over to the fire.

"Go away. I don't need any of your help with my fire. It's perfect." Grace raises the poker, and he backs up and laughs. "Just sit and behave."

Anne calls out to Emma from the porch. "Do you like s'mores? I have all the ingredients, unless, you're still too stuffed."

"Oh, I'm never too stuffed for s'mores," Emma responds from an oversized hammock strung between two towering poplars. She holds her library book above her head, reading it as she lies in that boneless way only young people can accomplish. Her notebook, which doubles as her journal, sits on the ground underneath her, a pencil marking her last spot. Having finished their examination of Seth, the dogs sprawl on the ground near her.

I settle into one of the chairs surrounding the fire area. Spike barely gives me time to sit before he's on my lap. I'm merely a vantage point for him to scope out Emma as he cleans himself. It's not long before he leaps down and saunters over to the dogs. He springs up, landing next to her. I watch him as he nudges her chin before he steps onto her and navigates his way to her stomach and begins kneading. As he lies down and resumes cleaning himself, she unconsciously pets him with her free hand.

Seth hands me the file, picks up the cat from the chair next to me, and settles down with him on his lap.

"Well, Sellis, open up that file, and let's see what we've got."

"Scoot your legs over, Grace, I'm going to sit here too." Anne carries a tray with s'mores ingredients, and a galvanized bucket filled with bottles. She sits next to Grace on a tree trunk bench. "I have cold beers for the grown-ups and a ginger beer for you, young lady."

"Yeah, Gram, I want to know if there are any more Victorian's in our family." Emma chimes in.

"What?" Seth asks.

"You know. You showed us the picture of Grandma Sophie when she was one. It starts with a v like a valet." Emma lifts her head up as she nods at me and widens her eyes. "Gram, you said they run in our family because you and my mom were vic, whatevers."

"Oh! Valedictorians. I'm sorry, Em. That's the word you're looking for." I look up from the papers on my lap at her.

"Victorian, valedictorian, valet, it makes perfect sense to me," Seth says.

"Hey, me, too," Emma and I say in unison.

"You two are funny. Emma, you're a lot like your Grandma. Is your mom anything like the two of you?" Anne looks between Emma and me as she passes around bottles of beer.

"My mom is the most serious person I know," Emma says. "She says Gram and I are fanciful dreamers, and not very practical."

All I can do is shrug because sometimes it's true. Holding up her bottle, Grace raises it in a toast. "Here's to all of us dreamers and the practical people who love us."

CHAPTER 12

The bonfire smells so much like home. I breathe, savoring the variety of emotions it brings. It's difficult right now to remember that I'm not at home. I shuffle through the stack of papers I've laid on my lap.

Concentrate Sellis. Breathe. Stay on track.

"So, are you all from here? Did you go to school together and hang out?" I ask.

"We are. Seth and I are cousins, and we'd see each other at family functions. Anne and I knew each other's names from school, but didn't hang out." Grace smiles at Anne.

Anne winks back. "And look at us now."

"Our families are what we call founding families. You'll come across our last names a lot as you read through our history books." Putting down her glass, Grace unbraids her sun-streaked, brown hair, then runs her fingers through it. I glimpse streaks of gray, which make me re-calculate her age. She's probably closer in age to me than I thought. Late forties? "So, I'll try to keep this short."

Anne smothers a laugh that becomes a snort.

"Whatever you say, Miss Queen of the Podium. As though you have the word short in your vocabulary. Especially on this subject." She lifts her glass in a toast to Grace as Seth laughs.

Grace grins in acknowledgment before she continues. "Where was I? Are you familiar with the Agrarian Movement? Our ancestors were there at the beginning. Eventually, they moved to the Midwest to start their own community. The core beliefs remain, even through changes and adaptations over the years."

I learn time operates pretty closely in both worlds. They have electricity but geothermal technology is their main energy source. We have a geothermal system at home, so I'm familiar with it. As a community, they've decided to limit the use of modern technology that we take for granted in our world, such as smartphones, the Internet, and television. They have Internet access in schools, clinics and hospitals, library and business places. In contrast, many private citizens have chosen to go without connections in their homes.

The way Anne and Grace explain it, this stance is a natural progression of their Agrarian philosophy. They're not averse to improving themselves and their lives. But they're not going to do so at the expense of damaging their natural environment.

One of the most critical and significant pieces of this world are the Guilds. They're an active and vital part of everyday life, blending traditions dating back to Medieval times and modern-day technology.

Anne rolls up her left sleeve so I can see the tattoo of a pineapple and a spiral surrounded by a heart. "I noticed your tattoo when you were washing dishes. Here's mine. The pineapple is a symbol of hospitality and welcome, which is part of what I do with the Fiddlehead, and the spiral represents my education in Celtic Studies. I've got my MBA, but Celtic Studies is my passion. I run the Fiddlehead using my business plan, and I remain part of the Celtic Studies program at our University system. I travel and learn and teach, plus I get to practice what I teach."

"We saw each other's tats at the library," Seth spoke up. "I told Sellis they've been part of our Guilds for a long time."

Anne's tattoo is lovely. And the similarity of her heart to mine gives me goosebumps.

"I know tattoos are common now, but they weren't when I got mine years ago. It's uncanny seeing Seth's tattoo and now yours. We all have the same heart symbol. I had no idea it was part of your culture. How could I? That feels like a magical coincidence."

We look at each other, and I smile at the thought of a bond that began long before we were born. The feeling I'd had about getting my tattoo had been so strong and unusual for me. Hearing about the tradition here through the years of getting one to celebrate a personal calling or craft makes perfect sense now.

"Sometimes a person knows from a very young age who they are and what they're meant to do with their life," Grace says. "And then there are those of us who find where we're supposed to be, purely by accident. I got my master's in theology and philosophy to teach and be a spiritual guide. When I was taking classes at the monastery, while I was doing kitchen duty, I fell in love with gardening and beekeeping. That led me down an additional path."

"Excuse me, ladies." Seth clears his throat and continues, "But, I think Sellis was asking about us and current events. I don't recall anyone asking for a history lesson."

"Let me tell this, Grace," Anne quickly says. "We'll be here all night if you keep on. Grace came to visit her family, and we ran into each other and connected. When my family home became available, we knew it was perfect for a bed and breakfast. Which turned out to be something each of us had dreamed of doing someday."

"Everything flows and happens the way it's supposed to, if you just let it," She laughs and bows her head, putting her hands together. "And how very Zen is that?"

Grace says, "Which goes to show, sometimes life doesn't go the way you think it will. I was just visiting family with no intention of staying. I thought I still had a lot of wanderlust in my soul. I certainly wasn't looking to fall in love and settle down, especially not in my hometown. I got offered a position at the school here in the Springs, and everything fell nicely into place."

Emma puts down her book and tunes in to our talk. "How many different tattoos are there? How do you know when it's time to get your tattoo? Do people ever have more than one?" Her pencil flies over the pages of her journal. I bet she's sketching ideas for her own tattoos.

"Each trade and craft has universal symbols, but there are new ones that show up all the time," Seth replies. "There are thousands of variations. They actually keep records of them at the guild headquarters. When it comes to knowing what your tattoo should be, it's a heart thing. You just have to take the time to listen. People get their tattoo when they get their degree or finish their apprenticeship, but we don't have any set rules."

"It's interesting that your Gram got a tattoo with a paw print and a heart entwined with ivy. I see that, and I know that she loves animals and plants," Grace gets up and turns my arm to look at my tattoo. She pushes up her sweatshirt to show me hers. "This is the Greek symbol for philosophy and, of course, the bee in honor of my hives."

"Gram should have a book there, too," Emma continues. "She reads even more than I do; Gramps always teases her about having to sleep with books."

Sitting back down, Grace continues, "You know, we meet a lot of people on quests. I think that's part of our easiness with you. We've all been on quests. Mine took me around the world before I realized this was right where I needed to be. Anne and Seth, on the other hand, always knew this was home, but there were other places and people they wanted to experience before they put down roots."

Seth, who has been sitting in his chair petting Bill, the cat, and listening, spoke up. "I think we probably have more travelers here in our world than yours. Life moves slower here, and I think it attracts a certain type of person. Sometimes it's easier to find answers and solutions here. Look at you, Sellis. You've found answers to questions here, that you've been carrying around for years."

Emma starts dozing off not long after eating a couple of s'mores, and I tuck her and Spike into their bed.

The papers Seth brought lay forgotten on my lap.

The more I hear, the more I like. The belief system here fits in with the path I've been walking on. I agree with Seth's statement that it's not just happenstance that I'm here. There's an air of familiarity around everything. I feel comfortable here. There's a sense of comfort between us, too. I know part of it is my Midwestern upbringing. It's more than that, though. I'm hesitant to say it, but it feels like coming home.

It's gotten closer to dawn than bedtime. I need to sleep, so I'm ready for what the day will bring. As comfortable as I am, I still have a growing sense of urgency about getting back on the road.

Seth left a couple hours earlier, shaking his head as he looked at his watch. "I have to say that this Tuesday was a lot more fun than they usually are. It's not every day that I meet a traveler that I'm related to. I can't wait to hear what you think about the information I gave you. Sellis, I know I'm going to see you and Emma and Spike again."

The light of the moon helps Anne and I tidy up while Grace takes care of the fire. "We talked so much you didn't get a chance to go through the papers Seth brought over," Grace says as she pours a bucket of water on the fire.

"It's okay. Finding out that Mom actually lived here, and was happy is more than I ever dreamed or hoped for. That gives me a whole new outlook on everything I knew or thought I knew about her. I came here not knowing anything about my mom, and now I can find out who she was." I hold open the door for them.

In the kitchen, they both hug me. "Sleep well. I know in my heart, you were meant to find us," Anne says.

"It's a homecoming. You not only found your mom, you found family." Grace squeezes me with tears in her eyes.

The heaviness behind my eyes tells me that my own tears are imminent. And I know without checking that my nose is already getting red. I can only nod through the tightness in my throat as I squeeze them both and hurry up the stairs to my room. I open the door with care and smile to see the two dogs snuggled against Emma, and Spike curled up under her chin.

CHAPTER 13

Bacon and coffee. Along with the tantalizing aroma, there are dishes clattering and voices murmuring. Nose and ears are awake, now I need my eyes and brain to catch up.

Where am I? Oh, yeah. The other Crystal Springs world.

Eyes open, I sit up and stretch. Emma and Spike are still entwined and asleep. No dogs, though. Good thing I left the door ajar.

A soft knock brings me to my feet. "Sellis, your owl is back. I just saw her fly into the trees by the garage." Anne holds up a cup. "I hope you like coffee. We can eat after you check on Tawny."

"Tawny's here? Gram, let's go see her." Emma and Spike are awake and on the move. The dogs come running at the sound of Emma's voice, barks turned up full volume.

And so the morning begins.

My braid is still intact, and our leather motorcycle jackets feel just right in the early morning chill. Standing by the garage, I softly call Tawny's name. "Hooo," she responds as she flies over to the roof above me.

"Hey, sweet pea, how are you?" I look her over as I

softly talk to her. "Did you have a good night? Come over here to me. Did you see Caleb? Are you hungry?"

Flying down onto the back of one of the wooden lawn chairs, she hoots at me as I walk over to her. I softly stroke the top of her head. She seems the same, with no injuries or differences that I can see. Maintaining my soft conversation, I check her jesses. Yes! Tawny made it home to Caleb, and he switched her jesses. He knows we're okay. The tightness in my chest loosens a bit. One less worry. I wish I could talk to him, but this helps. And if we get in trouble, I can use the black jesses and he'll know. Eventually.

"Thank you, Tawny, go take care of your owl business. Rest. Stay safe, sweet pea."

She flies off, and Emma and I do a quick celebration dance.

I send a quick prayer of thanks to the Universe. Caleb knows we're safe, and now I know Tawny can travel between our two worlds without using a portal.

This portal business is crazy. Anne, Grace and Seth are so nonchalant about it. Growing up using portals, wow. They don't even question the possibility that it might not work and we won't get home.

My mind leaps from portals to time. How long have we been gone? This is our third day gone, and our second day in this Crystal Springs. We're still on track, I'd planned to be gone for five days. Emma starts school next week, and Lily will be back this weekend.

I hadn't intended on taking our road trip this late in the season, but once again, life got in the way. My mid-summer break with Emma turned into this back to school trip, which isn't necessarily a bad thing except for the time of year. The autumn rains could come at any time, and I really want to avoid them. Riding in them can be ugly and dangerous; not something I want to do with Emma and Spike.

My stomach churns as I remember riding through sheets of rain so thick I couldn't see anything. I literally had to fight to keep my bike upright against cold, gusty winds pushing at me; trying to blow me off the road. At the same time I had to vary my speed because I needed to keep moving so the winds wouldn't buffet me around, but I couldn't go too fast or I'd start hydroplaning. My entire body ached when I was done. The memory of that ride still disturbs me and it's been years.

Anne and Grace meet us as we head back to the house. Tawny's journey between our two worlds is exciting news, and I also share my concerns about the rains.

They look at each other, and Grace says, "We might have something that will make your trip easier. Come into the garage."

Anne opens the garage door and walks over to an object covered by a tarp sitting next to their lawnmower. "Ta-Da!" she says as she pulls the tarp off a motorcycle sidecar. "How about if Miss Emma and Mr. Spike ride home in style?"

"Oh my gosh, Gram, this is the coolest thing in the world!" Emma shrieks as she runs over, climbs in, and sits down in it. "Will it fit on your bike? I could ride forever in here. I could sleep in here; I could live here." Her shadow, Spike, leaps gracefully onto the front of the sidecar and begins sniffing it as Emma continues her examination.

Incredulous, I walk over to the sidecar as Anne and Grace watch. I literally feel like I should pinch myself. My life feels surreal. Seriously, am I dreaming? Yes, it is the coolest thing in the world, and I really hope it fits my Trumpet too. What a blessing if it does.

"It belongs to my brother Sam. He's got a sixty seven Bonnie that he still rides, and it was made for that. He asked if he could store it here for a while, oh, about seven years ago," Anne tells me. "Now that I know you're interested, I'll let him know."

I look at her, and she smiles. "Grace and I talked about it last night, and I stopped by Sam's place this morning on my run. He's excited about meeting a fellow Triumph rider, and he said you can use it, if you're interested. He'll even hook it up for you."

"Of course, I'm interested! What a great idea, it's beautiful, it's a classic." I hug Anne to stop myself from babbling.

Back inside, I sit down at the table with my coffee cup and the folder Seth had brought me. Everything else fades away as I look through the pictures and the pieces of my mom's life that I never knew existed. Mom didn't talk about her childhood or family except for Grandma Flossie. Maybe she was the only family she had. I've never seen pictures of anyone else with Mom, only the one snapshot of her and Grandma Flossie I'd found with the fountain picture. My heart twinges as I think of the pleasure I saw on their faces. Why didn't Mom laugh more?

An official looking document turns out to be a copy

of a will naming Mom as Grandma's sole beneficiary. And then I come across a deed in both of their names.

"Hey, Anne, check this out." I walk over to her at the kitchen sink where she's cleaning vegetables. "Do you know where this is?"

"Hmmm. I don't. Seth will, though. You can run it over to him."

"I wonder if it exists in my world, and if it's in Mom's name there."

"I don't know why it wouldn't. It's yours now, Sellis. It belongs to you and your sister." Anne glances at me before concentrating again on the vegetables.

I wonder if Seth will have any luck tracking down the address. I scan through the rest of the papers and stop back at the newspaper article about Mom being named valedictorian.

I never knew anything about her. And she was my mom.

The sadness of this, and the loneliness of her life is heart wrenching on so many levels. Why? Why did she live like this? Why couldn't she share her life with us? I have so many questions and so much sorrow for her. I focus on the kitchen table, and Emma and Grace's conversation. Apparently they share a taste for current pop music.

Really? I'm having a hard time picturing Grace "shake it off." Huh.

Looking down, I see that I've spilled coffee. My hands tremble as I use my napkin to blot it up. Stacking the pages neatly, I place them back into the folder and turn my attention to the here and now.

I shower, and when I come downstairs, Grace has left for work, and Sam is here.

"I never felt right about getting rid of the sidecar after I took it off my bike," he shares. "My kids rode a lot of miles in it over the years, and I'm sentimental. I've had other bikes, but the Triumph was my first one. Annie's complained for years about it taking up space here, but now I know why I held on to it. Plus, Annie told me you're family, right?"

Sam and I go out to look at my bike and figure out what tools he's going to need.

"No problem. It'll work great and should only take a few hours." He's going to run home for tools and stop by his work, then he'll be back. I offer my help, but he tells me he's got it covered. "By the way, I like that you call her your Trumpet. It's a cool nickname for Triumphs, isn't it?"

I lean against my bike after he leaves and reflect on this new development. We need to get back to the fountain and through the portal, and that thought alone is causing me massive anxiety. Once we're through the portal, I'll get us home. No matter the weather. Once again, I feel the Universe helping me along. The sidecar is truly a gift.

I'm in our bedroom glancing through the papers again when Emma and her pack come sprinting up the stairs.

"Can we go over to Grace's school? Anne said we can take lunch to her and have a tour. And she said we need to drop something off at the library. I'm bored, and the dogs need a walk. Please?" Emma holds Spike's front paws inside her folded hands as she bows her head. The two dogs flank her, tails wagging furiously.

"That's a great idea. Let's go, gang."

"Yay!" The dogs bark in agreement as they all run downstairs.

I replace the papers in the folder and put it in my backpack, then follow at a slower pace.

"Here's Grace's lunch. Not that she'll take time to eat it, but I try." Anne hands me a cloth bag. "We can have a bite when you guys get back, and then tonight we'll grill. I think we'll all be in bed early after last night."

I nod as I tuck the bag in my backpack. "Yep, I'm too old for these late nights. I can't even remember the last time I stayed up like that."

"Gram, let's go." Emma and her pack are at the screen door.

"I need directions, hold on one sec." Smiling at Anne, I say, "Oh, to be young and filled with energy."

꩜

This Crystal Springs is no small town. The B&B is on the outskirts of a residential neighborhood. From the library, it takes us about twenty minutes to reach the school campus. I don't know why I'm surprised at its size. Grace called it a university, and it is.

Gee, it's got ivy-covered buildings and more gigantic trees.

Once again, Spike is my strolling companion as Emma and the dogs scurry ahead. I watch as they slow down to read another of the trademark, ornate signs. Emma motions towards the building when they turn onto the sidewalk. Trees tower above us as we walk up to the three-story brick building. It's quiet now, but school starts here next week too, so that will change.

"Animals are allowed everywhere here, isn't that cool?" Emma points to the sign on the door stating animals are welcome, please be considerate, and clean up as needed.

We find Grace's office on the main floor. She's been expecting us. She introduces us to her co-workers and then says, "Let's take a tour. I know you both will love our barns and the arboretum."

She's so right. Emma decides she's going to come back and go to college here; I want to, too. The greenhouse and science department is connected to the arboretum, and I could've stayed there for days. Obviously, the dogs had been on campus before because they were greeted everywhere we went, and they know where all the treats were.

Before we leave, Grace says, "I didn't forget about your mom. I've got a couple of resources I'm checking out and I'll bring whatever I find home."

I take my time back and marvel at this Crystal Springs. There are no similarities between the one in my world and this one, other than the names. I wonder why that is. Why did one world, realm (what do I call this place anyway?) thrive and grow, and the other one end up a ghost town? Was it really just the placement of a highway?

Walking up to the garage, I hear the sound of my bike. Wow. It looks like the sidecar was made for my Trumpet. I loved the classic black and chrome style of it before, and the sidecar emphasizes its timeless look. Sam looks extremely pleased sitting on it.

"Your timing is perfect," Sam grins at me and gets off so I can sit down. "I've tightened everything up and just got back. She feels good." Handing me my helmet, he tells me to take her around the block and see for myself. When I return, Emma is waiting with her helmet on, which makes me smile. That's my girl. She hops in, and we take a practice run. It's a different ride, but I can do it.

Anne comes out to the garage and admires the new look. "How about some lunch and then we can all ride out to Sam's brewery? You'll get some more practice and get to see his pride and joy."

Sam picks up his bike after lunch, and we all ride across town to where the Honey B. Brewing Company is.

"Oh, cool, you have your own bee hives right here. Oh. That's where the name comes from." Emma's delighted with the wordplay and then, amazed at the workings of the brewery. As am I.

Grace does come home with more papers and books to take with me. "I'm so excited about this, you guys. It's a listing of portals, can you believe it?" She hands me a notebook with a faded, thin cover. "I made copies of the pages but figured it would be more convenient for you to keep this tucked in your backpack. You can check these out in your world, and we'll keep track here and compare."

Duh. I never even thought about there being more portals. Of course there are. It's a huge world. I just can't believe I never knew about them before now.

Seth stops by with a more legible copy of Grandma Flossie's deed and an explanation about it's location. More research for me when I get home.

Reaching out, he clasps my hands in his. "Safe journey, Sellis. I look forward to seeing you here again."

Emma hugs him, thanking him for telling her about the book she'd read last night. "And thank you for the list of books you gave me. I can't wait to read them."

She holds one of Spikes paws up for a bump as he replies, "Have fun in school, Emma. You can give me book reports next time you visit."

It is an early night for all of us. The wind is blowing in from the west, and clouds are gathering. We're all in agreement that the rains are probably blowing in, too. It'll be another early morning for us so we can get on the road and stay ahead of the weather. Of course, I have no way of knowing what it'll be like once we go through the portal. All I can do is hope for the best.

Sleep doesn't come like I thought it would. Too many racing thoughts. So I go through our bags and get everything laid out and ready for the morning. Still unable to quiet my thoughts enough to sleep, I decide to go sit on the porch for a while. Wrapping a quilt around me, I head downstairs.

The cloud cover is hiding the stars and moon, and the wind carries a bit of an edge. I sit on the top step of the porch looking at the trees behind the garage, lost in my thoughts.

"Whoo. Whoo.".

Tawny! I didn't expect to see her so soon. Getting up, I walk over to the fence next to the garage.

"Hey, Tawny. Welcome." My heart lightens seeing her up in the trees. *I worry about you, sweet bird.* I lift my arm to signal her to fly to me, and she does, landing on the fence. "Hey, sweet pea. I'm so glad to see you." I softly touch her head while checking that her jesses are secure.

"Thank you, Tawny. Get rested. We've got another big day tomorrow."

I catch myself yawning as I watch her fly off. I'm finally ready to sleep. Tomorrow we're going home.

CHAPTER 14

I'm freezing.

Where the heck are the covers?

Curled on my side, in my usual sleeping style, I reach back for sheets, blankets, anything. Instead, I feel a blanket cocoon. That turns out to be my beloved grand-daughter wrapped up in all of the bedding. Which is typical behavior when I sleep with her. And yes, I'm right on the edge of the bed. Which is also typical. Emma, the bed and blanket hog.

"Let's go, Bright Ray of Sunshine." I sit up and give the blankets a tickle.

A slight breeze ruffles the sheers lining the bedroom windows. I can see the wind trees now, the sun will be up soon. Yep. The classic Big Ben style alarm clock on the nightstand shows "6:23." Shower and then caffeine to finish clearing my head.

꿍

I hate saying goodbye. I'm a whirling mass of conflicting feelings and racing thoughts. I keep reminding myself to "just breathe," but I'm not doing very well. There's such a strong pull inside me about this place AND these people. I've done such a thorough job of not thinking about my mom for so many years, it's weird to be acknowledging her and to actually be happy about it. I feel a weight has been lifted from my soul and a sense of completeness.

Honestly, I'm overwhelmed. But sort of okay with it.

We load up the bike dressed in our leathers and prepared for rain. The sky is overcast, and the local radio station has predicted rain. I have no way of knowing what the weather will be like once we go through the portal, but we'll be ready. Our rain suits and gauntlets are packed on top in the bags so I can access them fast if we need them.

Spike is draped across Emma's shoulders, his motor running loudly as he bats at the dogs milling around them. Tails wag double time as we pet them one last time.

Promises are made to return. "Knowing what I know, how can I not come back," I say. "I have a family here, and I need to learn the rest of my story. I feel like we're supposed to be part of this world in some way."

Grace nods, "You'll be back. I feel it in my heart."

Anne walks over and gives Emma a quick squeeze and smiles at me. I can see a glimmer of tears in her eyes.

Helmets, gloves, and sunnies on, I get Emma and Spike situated. Spike now has a willow basket to ride in on the floor. It's the perfect size for a cat carrier, with a split lid that flips up on both sides. He's snuggled in and content. Emma looks around and gives a beauty queen wave.

As I start up the Trumpet, she grins up at me. "Let's roll, Gram!"

"Ride safe. We'll see you soon." I faintly hear Anne and Grace over the bike and watch them waving at us in my rearview mirror. I'm glad I have to concentrate on driving because my emotions are revving up. You know that feeling when the tears are building up behind your eyes, and you know your nose is getting red? Yeah.

I concentrate on the road to keep those emotions buried. When we reach the fountain, I pull over and turn off the bike. Emma gives me a beauty queen wave and says, "This is the coolest thing ever. I can't believe we never had one of these before."

"It is cool, isn't it? I never needed a sidecar before; you're my first passenger. Okay, kiddo, let's go check out the fountain and go home."

After she climbs out, she reaches down and flips open the lid on Spike's basket. He springs out and dashes off. Shrieking, Emma rushes after him.

I call out to her as I pick up her helmet. "Emma, stop! Don't chase him. He thinks you're playing with him."

I take my water bottle from the bike bag and walk over to the fountain as I send a prayer to the Universe.

I'm scared. Please let this work.

Of course, it will work. But what if it doesn't?

Emma runs up, gasping for breath, as she holds on to Spike. "Here we are. Did you turn the water on yet?"

I open my water bottle. "Nope, I was waiting for you. I thought we could bring some water home for Gramps so he can taste it."

I hold the bottle under the faucet. We grab the handle together and flip it up. Water gushes out. When the bottle is full, we push the handle down together. I take Emma's hand as we turn around.

"It feels different, doesn't it? It's colder and not as big as it was before," she whispers. Her hand tightens on mine as she looks up at me with wide eyes.

She's right. It's changed again. The familiar North Dakota landscape rolls out in front of us. Everything does seem smaller, including the lake. The other shore is much closer, without tree-covered hills.

That "rain is imminent" smell is in the air, and I feel tingles on my skin.

It worked.

Kneeling down, I pull her next to me. "Yep, it does. That's good though, it means we're home."

I smile when I place the bottle of water in my bag, thinking about the story we'll share with Caleb. Tugging Emma's helmet strap tight, I watch her tuck Spike in, then we take off.

As I follow my tracks on the overgrown path, I see Tawny in my rearview mirror, ready to follow us home.

Forget what I said about our rolling hills. I forgot how steep this one is. Riding the bike up the hill is hard work. I miss the established roads in the other Crystal Springs. I try to stay in the tracks we left on our way down, but the side car's additional weight pulls me to the side. The Trumpet is a sturdy workhorse, though, and we slog up the hill.

By the time we finally make it to the top, I'm crabby and feeling overdressed in my leathers. I turn the bike off and take a deep breath undoing the strap of my helmet.

"Gram?" I look down at Emma's hesitant whisper.

Smiling, I reach my hand down. "I'm taking a breather, Emma before we go back to the highway. Give me a sec." Tawny swoops over us with a piercing, strident call interrupting me.

We both look as she soars up and flies away to the west. I see what she's trying to tell me. I'd been too busy watching the hill in front of me and hadn't been watching the skies.

A wall of thunderheads rolls towards us. Lightning strikes flash, and with the bike turned off, I hear the dull rumble of thunder.

The rains are here. Yes, the rains I hoped to avoid on our ride home.

I think over the route we drove to get here. It's about ten miles to the Interstate, and then the closest town is thirty miles. It's going to take us about an hour. There aren't any rest areas or gas stations in between, only a couple of exits leading to towns that are miles away. Farms along the way are tucked back, I wouldn't have time to find them.

I pull out my phone. Of course, there's no service.

Watching the storm clouds, I can't determine how fast they're moving. How do people calculate that anyhow? Am I foolish to even consider outrunning the storm?

For a brief second, I think about going back to the fountain and waiting out the storm in the other Springs. Nah. We'll be fine.

As long as the weather holds off, I can do this.

Getting off the bike, I pull out our rain suits. Emma has been keeping a close eye on me and doing an excellent job of staying quiet as I work through this situation.

Now the questions fly.

"Are we going to ride into that storm? Can lightning strike us? Will I keep totally dry in my rain suit? What about Spike? He's going to get wet in his basket."

She's climbed out of the sidecar by the time I have the rain suits. Following my lead, she pulls the packaging off and shakes the jacket and pants to get out the wrinkles. She starts giggling.

Her eyes roll when she holds it up to herself. "This looks like a muumuu. Why is it yellow? And why is it so long?"

"I don't want to lose you in a rainstorm. Yours is big for you; you'll be able to use it for a few years. Spike will be fine. We'll push him all the way to the front of the sidecar, and he'll stay dry in his basket." I know my voice is tight, and my comments are clipped, so I add a silly comment to make her groan. "MuuMuu along my bright ray of sunshine."

It works. A few tucks and shakes, and we're ready. Looking to the west, I see the cloud bank has inched closer.

"Those clouds are ginormous. They cover the whole sky, Gram."

I'm now officially a nervous wreck. Thank goodness, there's no wind or rain.

Yet.

Just that ominous heavy feeling in the air and in my gut.

I hold onto Emma a few seconds longer after I help her into the sidecar. We get Spike's basket snugly situated, so he's safe.

"Let's roll," we say together as we take off.

It's not long before I know we don't have an hour before the storm hits. I didn't take into account that I'm not moving as fast now because of the sidecar. We're at the Crystal Springs exit, ready to pull onto the Interstate. I'm going over my options.

I pull out my phone.

Ta! Da! I have service!

And I have a weather alert. Severe thunderstorms and a tornado warning. Oh, really? All of the words that I tell Emma she can't use are flying through my head. I feel like a foolhardy idiot and a terrible person for putting us in this scary predicament.

Emma sings a song to Spike. Her words about storm riders drift past me. Taking my eyes away from the mesmerizing thunderhead coming towards us, I glance behind.

The two-story brick schoolhouse is visible through the cottonwood and poplar trees. A lot of the upper windows are broken or boarded up. Thinking back, I remember a couple of outbuildings and even an enclosed stairwell we might be able to take shelter in.

It's our only chance, so I don't waste any time.

Emma's eyes are enormous as I do a u-turn. We go across the overpass and head to the school. Splashes of rain run down my helmet visor, and the wind plucks at my rain suit. A gust pushes us as we drive across the grass in front of the school.

I spot the stairwell just as the rain changes from scattered drops to a steady drizzle.

Seriously? Can't I get five minutes here?

As we drive around the corner of the school, it blocks the wind and rain a bit. Pulling up to the school as close as I can, I park the Trumpet. I get off my bike, not even bothering to remove my helmet and gloves.

We're out of time.

Emma is sitting ramrod straight, and I see her lips moving. I reach down and lift up her visor.

"Honey, we're gonna be fine. Grab Spike's basket and get out, okay? We're going into the stairwell."

I dash over to the wooden structure that's not much more substantial than a lean-to. Missing boards mar the weather-beaten, grey wood walls. At least I don't have to worry about getting in, as the door is wide open and clacking back and forth in the occasional wind gusts. The concrete steps are relatively clean and dry. It's light enough to see no one else (human or animal) is seeking shelter inside.

I hold the door open for Emma, then go back to the bike for our backpacks and the insulated bag with waters and snacks. The last things I grab are two mylar space blankets that I've carried around for years for emergencies. Windproof, waterproof, and warm. Just what we're going to need.

CHAPTER 15

I slip my boot around the ajar door and try to pull it towards me. The rain is now a steady deluge, and I'm grateful for my rain suit. Lightning cracks right behind me, and the instant boom of thunder makes me wonder just how close it came. A gust of wind catches the door and pushes me back.

"Emma, can you open the door for me?"

She runs up the steps shining her pocket flashlight in one hand while she holds Spike with the other.

"Gram, I could see into the school through the door, and I think we can get inside." She slides behind me and stands next to the door holding it open.

Lightning streaks across the sky, and the thunder is a continual rumble. Spike leaps down, Emma shrieks, and I lose my grip on the insulated bag with our goodies. It tumbles down the steps alongside Spike.

Ha. Who needs thunderstorms when I have my own personal special effects factory? Emma's hair gets soaked when her hood is blown back, and gusts threaten to pull her away. With my free hand, I grab hold of her rain suit and pull her inside. She races down the stairs after Spike, who stops at the bottom to investigate the door. I wrestle with the door and succeed in pulling it closed. The wind gusts are growing more intense, and I have my doubts about how long it will stay closed, or even attached.

There are missing boards in the roof, too. In fact, this isn't a particularly sturdy or protective shelter. Especially not in this storm. It's still dryish at the bottom of the stairs. Standing next to Emma and Spike, I set down our packs. Using my wet raincoat sleeve, I try to rub off some of the accumulated grime on the metal door's window.

Emma jiggles the door handle and looks over her shoulder at me, "See, it turns. I think you're strong enough to open it. And the door is bent. I think we can pull it open."

Another clap of thunder leads to a renewed torrent of rain.

Shoot. We're going to get flooded out of here if this keeps up, and I have no reason to believe it won't.

"Let me see, Em. You two scoot back into the corner where it's drier." I hand her the towel I use to dry off the bike. "Here, you can use this to dry your hair and Spike, if he'll let you."

Sure enough, the handle does move. I don't think it's locked either. Putting my weight on it, I work at pulling it down. I can move it, but the door sticks where the wooden frame has swollen. It's an emergency exit door made to open outward, so I can't even try to push it. If only I had something to stick into the cracks and pry it open.

Ah ha. My buck knife may just earn its keep again today. Pulling it out, I think I can even keep it in its leather sheath and still get it into one of the gaps between the door and frame. Now, if only I'm strong enough.

I haven't noticed how dark it's become as I concentrate on opening the door. "Hey, Em? Can you shine your flashlight over here, please? What's that song you're singing? Can you sing louder, I can't hear you."

I know she's singing because she's scared. Hopefully, singing to me will distract her.

It's tedious and slow-going, and my fingers are numb from trying to pry the door open. I have no idea how much time has passed, but because I can barely hear her, I know Emma's losing her voice, or the storm is getting worse.

"Gram!"

The door flies open, the stairwell lights up, and my ears pop from a crack of thunder. Emma and Spike are behind the door. I pull it away from them. "Take Spike, and get inside." She darts past me, and I pick up our bags and follow her.

Water is pouring through every hole in the walls and roof of the lean-to. The very walls are shuddering as the wind picks up. The lightning is a giant non-stop strobe light, and the thunder is a dull continual roar.

I set my backpack next to Emma and turn back to the open door. "Please get my flashlight. I think we'll need both of them in here."

The bottom of the stairwell is filling with water. I swear the wind has gotten stronger, along with the amount of rain coming down. There are moments that I'm hanging on the door because my feet have slipped out from under me.

Please. Give me strength. I can do this.

Finally, I manage to get a good grip on the handle and can pull it shut. Years of weather and settling don't allow it to seal, but I'm not complaining. I would never have gotten it open if it had been closed properly.

The windows are mostly boarded over, and our flashlights are the only source of light. The sound of thunder is ongoing, along with the steady downpour of rain. The force of the wind makes it sound like sheets of rain are being tossed against the walls.

"Hey, you two, come over here." I motion Emma over to me. "Let's get out of our rain suits and then take a look at this place." It might be a mistake taking off the suits, but they're more of a hassle now. I shake them out and roll them up as best I can.

I take out my flashlight and shine it around. We're in a cavernous, mostly-empty room. Exposed pipes among the wooden beams above us have cobwebs hanging from them. The school has been vacant for such a long time, anything of value or use is long gone. There's an untidy pile of wood scraps and a couple of old desks and chairs next to some wooden crates.

I could have used one of those pieces of lumber to pry that door open.

I walk over and check out the chairs. They're dusty but sturdy enough, so we don't have to sit on the floor. I stop when I notice Emma is shivering.

"Let's drag the chairs and a couple of crates over by the wall where we'll be safe from the wind and rain. Kind of like a fort, okay? I think it's time we sat down and had a snack and some water."

Fortified with banana chips and a bottle of water, Emma wraps one of the mylar blankets around herself and Spike. I cram the rain suits into the space left in the bag and continue my exploration. Pulling a desk below a window, I hop up and look out through a space between the boards.

The rain is coming down so densely I can't see anything. In the seconds after a lightning flash, I see the ground is covered with running water. The thunder and lightning haven't decreased at all.

I cannot imagine being caught outside in that.

"Spike, no! Come here!" Emma shrieks.

Turning my head, I see Spike leap off a bucket covering a pipe sticking out of a wall. The clattering of the bucket is loud in the sudden silence.

What?

Why would the storm all of a sudden be silent?

And what is that pipe that Spike uncovered? Some sort of well?

Oh, my gosh, my ears just popped. It's not quiet anymore. I'm afraid of what that loud roar means. I think it's a tornado.

CHAPTER 16

Rumbles, thuds, cracks surround us. Are the walls crumbling down? Seconds ago, it was hard to take a deep breath, it felt like the air was sucked away. My breaths are shallow now. I could taste the quiet on my tongue, now it's thick and gritty. The noise pummels me now, thumps and thuds so loud they're palpable, solid. My ears hurt, and I'm on my knees. Looking up, I see part of the reason for the racket. Above me, the wood has been torn off the windows, and pieces swirl like leaves in a breeze. Though ever-growing gaps in the walls and ceiling, I see a mass of light grayish colored clouds roiling across the dark sky. The schoolhouse is imploding around us.

"Emma!" I look over at the wall where she had been seconds earlier. There's so much dust and debris flying around, I can't see anything. I'm dizzy from the non-stop lighting flashes. I crawl over to where she had been, calling out her name, even though I can barely hear my own voice. I move one hand back and forth in front of me as I crawl, hoping to come into contact with something.

Where is she?

I touch leather, and a small hand grabs mine.

Oh, thank God.

Tears roll down my face as I scoot over to her and pull her close. We inch along together until I feel the rough concrete wall. The sound of the thunder is a continual dull boom, so I can't explain what I'm trying to do. Flashes of lightning allow me to see enough to clear us a place. Emma slides down and wraps her arms around her knees. I murmur into her hair, hoping she can hear me, but I doubt it. With my arms wrapped around her, I feel every sob and breath she takes.

The wind howls. Rain and rubble swirl above us. I watch in horrified fascination as a sheet of plywood swoops down and narrowly misses us. It crashes next to us. Something roars in my ears, and my breath is sucked away.

I push against the board with my shoulders, and Emma and I scoot underneath it. Moving Emma as close to the wall as I can, I cover her with my body and pray that the plywood protects us.

What is tickling my nose? I can't move my arms to brush it away. I can't see a thing. I'm wet. And cold. What is going on?

Prrrrrr. I recognize that purr. It's Spike. Sitting right in front of me. If he's here, I must be alive.

My attempts at moving have inspired Spike to become active. In the darkness, I feel him nudge me. He moves on, over to Emma. Loose strands of her hair are plastered on my face tickling me. I blow and manage to get them off. One of my arms is under Emma, who's scrunched between me and the wall. Our plywood savior has now become our jailer. I'm pinned and can barely move. I feel her chest move, but I don't know if she's awake since she's not answering me.

"Are you okay?" Trying to move my arms isn't working, so I try my legs. She's curled up in a fetal position in front of me, and I'm spooning her. Hey, I can move my legs. Slowly I try to straighten them as I continue talking to her, trying to get her to respond. She's breathing, but I can't tell if she's asleep or unconscious.

Spike has moved over to her head, and his purrs grow louder as he kneads her shoulder. If that doesn't get a response, I will be genuinely worried.

I touch the wall with my boots, and, bracing them, I push.

Success.

I'm able to roll back enough to shift the plywood and move my top arm. There must be something on top of it.

Think, woman. You can figure this out.

We're not crushed, I'm able to wiggle, but Emma's not responding at all to Spike or me. I've got to get us out of here.

With my feet braced against the wall now, I push up with my hips. There's resistance at first, but I manage to get the plywood to start sliding. I feel the weight shifting as something slides off with a thud, and I hear things rolling. One more big push and the plywood pops up, and so do I.

It's pitch black again now that the gigantic mass of clouds is gone. Water drips on me, we're lying in a freezing pool of it. I think the roof is gone, yet I can't see a thing.

"Gram, where are you?"

Hearing her voice makes me giddy with relief.

Kneeling, I wrap my arms around her. We're both trying to talk at the same time, which is hard to do when you're crying. Spike is trying to wrangle his way between us, so I sit down and pull them both on my lap.

Words spill out in between sobs and sniffs. "What happened to us? Where are we? Am I blind? Why can't I see?"

"We're okay. We're still in the basement. I think there was a tornado. I don't know why it's so dark. I wish I could find a flashlight."

She reaches into her jacket. "Here, Gram." Handing me her mini Maglite, she whispers, "I have to remember to thank Gramps for giving me this and telling me to always keep it with me because you never know when you might need a light."

"Very true. We'll both thank Gramps." Turning it on, at first, I don't understand what I'm seeing.

There's no building on top of us.

We're in the basement, but most of the ceiling, and the two floors above it, are gone, and there's nothing but rain and sky beyond it. There's a chunk of the roof? flooring? directly above us, but the remainder looks more like a pergola. That piece of plywood was our saving grace. The section where we are is relatively bare, but the rest of the basement is covered with bricks, boards, and tree branches. *Oh my gosh, I see my backpack.*

Emma has started shaking with cold again.

I need to get us out of here and someplace safe.

"I'm going to get your sweatshirt, and then we'll get out of here."

Standing up, I see the mylar blanket crumpled under the plywood. I pull it out and wrap it around Emma. Spike is no longer on her lap, but I can hear him as I work on freeing my backpack.

Searching with the flashlight, I find him in an empty gap where a window once was. "What's going on, buddy?"

Gingerly making my way to him, I turn over the desk that had been on top of us and stand on it.

Oh.

It's not only the school that's gone. Everything is gone.

CHAPTER 17

The rain has slowed to a steady mist, and the landscape is blurry. I don't recognize anything I see. I've never seen devastation like this in my life before. The few buildings that were here last week have disappeared. As have the trees. Nothing breaks the endless expanse of flatness.

It's so dark. A sudden flash of lightning and the responding thunder boom startle me as I look outside. The sky is still filled with rain and clouds, with no stars or moon visible. How much time has passed? What time is it?

Oh! My phone. Where is it?

As I unzip the pocket I keep it in, I keep looking for anything recognizable. A heartfelt, one-word prayer flashes through my thoughts.

Please.

Pulling out my phone, I push the home button.

It lights up, but so do those infamous words - "no service." I'm not surprised.

Wait a minute. My bike. What if…

No. No. No.

Think. What side of the building did I park it on?

I turn around on the desk, sweeping the room with my light, to get my bearings. When I find the door, I figure out where the Trumpet should be.

The wind gusting through the open space sprays me with a fine mist of rain. Which makes me realize I'm wet. Wetter than I would be from the storm blowing in on me.

Oh, right. We were lying in water when I woke up or came to. Could all of the water on the floor come from losing the roof? Hmmm. There's water coming out of that pipe Spike jumped on earlier. I wonder where that's from. No wonder we're soaked and Emma's shivering.

I get off the desk and reach for Spike, who had followed me onto the desk. He avoids my hands and dashes over to Emma as I cautiously make my way to my backpack. Water drips non-stop on me, and I slosh through standing water as I make my way through pieces of lumber and pipes. Looking up, I have no explanation for why we're okay. I see a lot of open space above me compared to ceiling, and the only clear area on the floor is where we were.

Spike is purring and rubbing his head against the burrito-wrapped Emma. Crouching down, I lift the blanket piled on top of her head. Emma blinks and peers at me. Brushing her bangs to the side, I lean over and kiss her forehead.

She feels clammy, and her skin is cold.

I've got to warm her up. We've got to get out of here. Fast.

"Hey, sweetie, Spike wants to snuggle with you."

Reaching into my backpack, I hand her a sweatshirt. "Let's put this on over your jacket. It's one of Gramps, so it's big. I'm going to look outside, but I won't be long. You stay here and take care of Spike for me."

"I'm thirsty and freezing." Coughing and then sneezing, she continues. "What happened? Where are we?"

I help her pull the sweatshirt on and answer as I give her a pair of socks. "We're in the basement of the school. I think there was a tornado, but we're okay."

"What are these for?"

"Fuzzy gloves to help you warm up."

The side-eye I get is a good sign.

"Okay, you've got Spike, and here's some water. I'm going to wrap you back in the blanket, and you two hang out. Did you know you looked like a giant burrito wrapped up in this thing?"

A soft giggle followed by a round of coughs is her response.

After the two of them are snuggled in, I re-braid my hair and put my cap on for whatever protection it may offer from the rain. Flashlight, phone, and buck knife; I'm ready.

Before I go, I take one more look around the room. It would've been so much easier to go through that door, but the rubble piled in front makes that impossible. Nope, the window is our only way out.

Rain continues to come through the window. This place is getting wetter by the minute.

Back up on the desk, I shine the light outside. I can pull myself up and over the window sill, and then it's only a few feet to the ground.

Flashlight and phone securely zipped up; I pull myself onto the ledge without too much trouble. *Thank God for*

Pilates and core strength. And adrenaline. Dropping to the ground, I'm surprised at the soft, muddy ground when I land. Reaching out, I put my hand on the wall to get my balance and look around. It's too dark to see anything. Pulling out my flashlight, I get a good look at - emptiness.

Pretty much nothing is left standing.

A flash of lightning confirms that and also shows me the corner of the stairwell. I need to go around that, and my bike should be over there.

God willing.

The wood structure over the stairwell is gone.

I feel like I've been punched in the stomach when I see the open stairs. There's not a single piece of lumber left, and the steps are totally bare. Not a twig or leaf on them, only water Like a super vac came through. We wouldn't have survived if we hadn't been able to get inside.

My feet are dragging as I walk to the corner. I'm so afraid of what I'll find. Or not find. But my thoughts are racing. So many possibilities.

Please. Please. Please.

I find the remains of the wooden stairwell shed. They're scattered around in various-sized pieces. Some of them landed on the Trumpet.

My bike is still here! And it looks intact.

"Thank you!" Shouting and singing, I splash my way to the Trumpet and start grabbing pieces of wood. With my mantra of thanks on repeat, I gather and toss. I walk around the bike and check it out. There are a couple of dents and scratches. I say another prayer of thanks. She's still here! The sidecar is secure, there's some water standing in it, but nothing I can't scoop out.

Okay. Now the big test. Will she start?

Of course, she does.

Head bowed, tears falling and mixing in with the rain, I'm lost in a prayer of thanks.

Until I feel the Trumpet quiver.

What?

Tawny is sitting on the sidecar.

"Whoo."

And then my phone starts vibrating.

Tawny watches me as I fumble with the zipper on my jacket and finally get my phone out. Oh. Weather alerts about a potential tornado.

Thanks for that.

Since I have it out, and it's working, I dial Caleb's number. It rings and rings and rings. I guess service isn't totally restored.

I look back at Tawny and send her a mental hug since I can't physically hug her. Having her show up inspires me and gives me hope. If she can fly and get around, so can we.

I turn off the bike and finish cleaning off the Triumph. One last task and we can get moving. I need to see what the ground is like and if I can drive away from here on it. The rain is more of a drizzle, which is good. The storm has to be almost done.

I'm soaked. I want to go home.

A hoot from Tawny stops me, and I look over as she takes off. She swoops down and lands on a chunk of the school wall.

"Hoot."

I hear the faint response from inside.

"Whoo are you?"

Emma's awake.

Laughing to myself, I give the Trumpet one last glance.

"Hey, gang, let's roll!"

CHAPTER 18

By the time I get back inside, I'm seriously questioning my ability to get us out of here. My initial burst of energy and strength didn't last long. Cross fit just might get placed higher on my list of goals after I'm home. What I wouldn't give for more upper body strength right now.

Pulling away the blanket draped over Emma, I brush aside her hair. She's clammy, and her clothes are damp underneath her jacket.

Her sparkle is fading.

The delight I heard in her greeting to Tawny is gone when she says, "I'm freezing and thirsty. I don't want this yucky water. I want some lemonade." She looks up at me and bursts into tears. "These socks are dumb, I can't feel anything with them on. I want my mittens."

Oh, snap.

This whiny little girl is not my personal ray of sunshine. This is a sick child.

Change of plans.

She needs to get warmed up, so I head back to the bike for dry clothes. Soon she's wearing more layers and has another bottle of water to drink. My anxiety level notches up because, after that initial outburst, she's silent. I want my inquisitive, firecracker girl. I rewrap her in the space blanket, this time with her sitting up on a chair.

My adrenaline kicks in again, fueled now by fear for Emma. I find a rhythm to my trips back and forth to the bike. Years of packing my Trumpet help, and I operate on auto-pilot. There's not as much water sitting in the side-car as I feared, and I'm grateful for the leather seat in it.

"Bzzzzp. Bzzzzp."

What? Oh, geez, my phone is vibrating. I feel it only because I'm laying on it as I pull myself over the window ledge for what seems like the five hundredth time. I straddle the ledge, take a deep breath, and slide down onto the desk. I pull it out of my pocket. *Please let it be Caleb.*

Oh yay. Two alerts. Severe weather warning and my battery is low.

Too bad shaking the phone doesn't do anything.

"Hey, burrito girl, let's get going. Spike and Tawny want to get home tonight." As I reach down and unwrap the blanket, I have to stop myself from gasping.

What is going on with Emma?

Her summer tanned face is a pasty white, and her hair is clumped and damp. *Maybe her fever broke.* I pull her up and wrap an arm around her waist to keep her standing. Her eyes are blinking, and they finally open, but are unfocused. I keep up a stream of mindless comments and platitudes. One slow step at a time, we make our way. An unwavering prayer is on repeat inside me. *Please, let her be okay, just let me get her home. Please keep her safe.* It feels like forever getting her up onto the window ledge and outside into my arms.

She immediately drops to her knees. "I'm so tired. I'll just lay down and wait here, okay."

Bending over, my hands go under her arms to pull her up.

I'm so afraid.

I wrap my arms around her and try not to cry as I carry her to the Trumpet.

"Whooo. Whooo."

Tawny startles me when she swoops in front of us and flies over to the Trumpet. Spike joins her by jumping onto the sidecar while meowing loudly. What I wouldn't give to understand cat and owlese.

"What? I know she's sick. I'm moving as fast as I can. I'm going to get her home."

They're both agitated, but why?

I look around and don't see any changes in the nothingness around us. A light mist tickles my exposed skin. The clouds are a thick rolling blanket above us. The moon is full and peeks through every now and then, which is a godsend.

Emma is helmeted and buckled in, and I get Spike into his somewhat soggy basket. Tawny continues to fly back and forth between the school and us, as though she's trying to tell me something. One last time before we head off, I pull out my phone. It's after midnight. How did that happen? I try Caleb's number one last time, even though the phone has no bars. My battery is almost dead. Kinda like my personal battery.

Thank goodness the Trumpet's battery is in working

order! The familiar growl as I start it up revives my spirits, and I glance down at Emma. "Let's roll."

No response from my girl. How I miss her usual grin and thumbs up.

It's surprising how little debris there is as I drive away from the school. I carefully navigate my way through standing water. Tawny has disappeared again, and the empty landscape is freaking me out. How can there be nothing left? Where did the trees and plants and grass and everything go? Looking around, I don't see anything. No lights. No buildings. No hills. No stars. Nothing.

Past the school, I come to a gravel road. Something is wrong. It only goes to my right. East. Did I get turned around? Where's the one back to the Interstate? The one we came in on. I don't see it. All I see is this road. I can't see anything beyond the light from my bike.

What is going on?

Suddenly, Tawny lands on the ground about ten feet in front of the bike. I stop and sit there looking at her, wishing so badly I could understand her. "What's going on, Tawny? What are you trying to tell me?" Her response is to fly down the road. In what I know is the opposite direction of the Interstate and home.

Oh my gosh. My hands slip off the handgrips, and the Trumpet shuts off. Turning my head to look where Tawny flew off, I figure out what she's trying to tell me.

Somehow, in the storm or because of it, we ended up somewhere else. This isn't my Crystal Springs. I don't know if it's Mom's, but now I know what Tawny's trying to tell me. We can't go that way. Home's not there. There's only one way to go.

This road has to lead to the fountain just like it has before. If there's any logic here, it'll be in the same place here, too. Once again, the fountain is the key.

CHAPTER 19

Tawny is back. She loops around me in her silent owl stealth mode. "Okay, Tawny. Now that I've figured out what you were trying to tell me, what's next? Where are we? Oh, how I wish you could tell me if what I'm thinking is right."

I place my hands back on the handgrips but don't start the Trumpet. I blink away tears of frustration or fear, or whatever they are. I draw myself a map of Crystal Springs in my head. Based on the previous two worlds, this one has to have a similar layout, right? If only I had more light...

Viola! I wasn't paying attention. The cloud cover isn't as heavy as it was. Yay! Ahhh. There's the moon, and I swear it's glowing. Okay. I'm maybe a bit giddy right now seeing the moon. It is lovely, and I can see past the Trumpet. Yep, I was headed the right way. There's the road.

It's the only road. This road only goes back the way we came. There is no other road. No road that leads over to the Interstate.

What? Where's the road that goes to the Interstate?
Tawny hoots as she glides away.

"Got it, Tawny. We're coming."

Emma hasn't stirred. Part of me is afraid to touch her or check on her. I've done all I can do for now to keep her safe.

I start the Trumpet, and it's a bumpy, wet ride. In the moonlight, I can see a lot more water than I expected to on the ground. When we reach the road, it's gravel, no pavement at all. Ha. I don't know if this is even a gravel road. It's more of a two-lane prairie path.

Any doubts I'd had are gone. This is definitely not the same place we came to before the storm.

I'm just going to stop thinking and drive.

The additional light from the moon and stars shining above help me feel more at ease. I don't see Tawny anywhere, though. There are scattered trees and tall grass alongside us. We're going east, I've been here a few times now, it should start looking familiar.

Finally. I remember this hill. When I reach the top, I look down, and there's the lake. Cottonwoods of varying sizes cover the land around it. Again, it's a different body of water. It looks more like a slough surrounded by tall grasses. Nothing looks familiar. Where's the fountain? It's supposed to be right down there.

I find a level spot and park. I look down at Emma. She's asleep. It's so quiet with the bike turned off, I can hear soft little snores.

This is a good sign.

No sounds from Spike's basket, so I'm going to leave the two of them here and go check things out. I should be able to hear vehicles from the Interstate, or geese or something. There's nothing, only a deep quietness that bothers me. Where is everyone? Why aren't there any traffic sounds?

Caleb's flashlight shines strong. *Thank you, thank you, thank you. These little guys have definitely been lifesavers.*

It's a slow hike down the hill. Trees and saplings of varied sizes surround me, and the grass and brush are thick and, at times, waist-high. There's no path to follow, and I'm thankful I have my leathers on. My boots sink into mud, and I squish with every step. There's no beach, just this gradual slope. I'm at the edge of the lake. I turn in a circle, trying to find the fountain.

Oh, my gosh. There's a pile of rocks, and I think I see a pipe with a basic pump with a handle set on top of it.

I scramble across the grass. Yes. Water is dripping down the spout, and there's a pool of water below in a natural made pool.

When did Anne and Grace say the fountain was built? 1930's, I think. Man, this must be the original fountain. It should still be a portal, right? But what year is this?

Bottom line is the water. I can't mess this up. Based on what happened at the school, the water is how we go from one place to another. Obviously, the pipe Spike discovered in the old school had been connected to the spring and was also a portal. The seal keeping it closed was leaking when we got there, and it broke all the way. That's how we got here, wherever this is.

Should we stay here and try and find people? I have no idea how I could even explain anything about this situation. That doesn't seem like a good idea.

If I just cup my hands under the water, is that going to be enough? Are Emma and Spike close enough? The bike

118

went with us before, and it wasn't right beside me, but Emma and Spike always were.

"I don't know what to do!" My voice is a whisper.

"Whooo. Whoooo."

"Gram!"

Emma and Tawny's cries startle me, and I slip and fall onto the rocks.

CHAPTER 20

I am going to stop saying that I will bounce if I fall because of the padding on my butt. It is not true. I don't bounce regardless of the amount of padding that I have. And it doesn't have to be icy to slip and fall. Was I knocked out again?

My eyes open, and I shake my head, but immediately stop because it feels like someone is pounding stakes into my brain.

Whoo! Whoo!

Everything comes rushing back to me when I hear Tawny. I remember Emma called out, and Tawny hooted. And then I slipped.

The sun is coming up. This dreadful, never-ending night is coming to an end. I take a breath and sit up. Ouch. It hurts. I hurt everywhere. Okay. Time to open my eyes.

I see Tawny.

I'm on the rocks in the water, in front of the fountain pipe. Tawny is perched on the pipe gazing down at me.

"I'm coming Emma." My voice croaks, and I try again. The simple act of clearing my throat makes my head throb. My hands are blocks of ice, and water drips from them when I check it out. I feel a nice lump on the back of my head under my matted and smushed hair.

How long was I out? What is going on? I have to get up to Emma.

I don't hear any sound from her, which kicks me into overdrive. My body is not responding to my request to move. Ha. Not that I might have overdone the physical activity thing today. Yesterday. Whatever.

I wonder what time it is. At least it's not raining anymore.

Another hoot from Tawny stops my wandering thoughts. And then, as if in response, I hear what sounds like a wolf howl. I watch Tawny glide up the hill as I stand up. *Just breathe.* My steps are slow and cautious as I make my way back across the rocks. "Emma, I'm coming." My voice works, and my legs get steadier as I go.

My heart stops when I reach the top and see a person and a dog or is it a wolf, standing next to the Trumpet. There's no sign of Tawny, but now I know where the howl came from. Either that's a wolf or a wolf cross watching me.

"Hey, who are you? What do you want?" I forget my aches when I go into Mother Bear mode. *Who is this? Is Emma okay?*

Dressed in baggy trousers and a canvas barn coat and work boots, it's a woman with her hair pulled back in a loose braid. She walks around the bike, extending her hand as she speaks. The dog that looks like a wolf stays right by her side, mirroring her. "I'm sorry to startle you. My name is Flossie. Are you okay? I was just coming down to check on you. Your girl is running a temperature."

I brush past her, focused totally on Emma.

"Please don't be alarmed. I mean you no harm. I live down the road. The sound of your machine and your lights woke me. It is very late, or very early, I guess you could say, so I came to investigate." She's got a British accent and enunciates each word, as though she's unsure I'll understand her.

I stopped paying attention after I heard her say that her name is Flossie.

Flossie? My Flossie? What is going on? How many Flossie's can there be? What is happening?

I bend over the sidecar, placing my hand on Emma's forehead. She is indeed burning up. Straightening up, I take Flossie's hand.

"Thank you. I'm sorry if I'm distracted. I fell on the rocks, and then I heard Emma and Tawny, and now here you are…"

She squeezes my hand before she lets go as she says, "We should look at your injuries and cool your girl down. Please let me offer you assistance at my home."

Her speech is formal or old-fashioned, just like her clothing. And the thought that her name is Flossie is freaking me out. But I'm not going to turn down her offer of help. What choice do I have?

"Please, yes - I would very much appreciate any help you can give us." My words are stilted and forced. It's like my brain is frozen. I can't think.

I stand still as Flossie pats the Trumpet, shaking her head, and then tilts her head with a smile. "Follow me on your motor contraption. If I fall behind, keep going into the sunrise. You'll know when you arrive at my home. It's not far, perhaps half a kilometer from here."

"It's a motorcycle. I'm sorry I don't have room for you. Do you have cars here?" I sputter, and my face is on fire, but I finally stop blabbing. Flossie touches my shoulder as she goes past me, her wolf cross by her side. She looks back and smiles, which reminds me to move.

What is happening? Where are we? Is that really Grandma Flossie? And she has a pet wolf? It's gotta be a farm dog, like Daisy. Somewhere in there a wolf stopped by, but it can't be a full wolf. Can it?

My thoughts race as I nod my head and remember that I actually need to move my body. Fifteen years of riding serve me well; habits ingrained take over since I'm not thinking.

I double-check that Emma's strapped in and her helmet is secure.

"Hey, Spike, how are you doing?" A quick meow and a scratch on his basket tell me he's okay. "Hold on, buddy, you'll be out of there soon."

Helmet plopped on, gloves pulled on, I turn the key. Here I go. Attentive, watchful, and careful, I drive back onto the road. Flossie is in sight but moving faster than I thought she would.

How did I make it down this road in the dark? Thank you again for watching over us.

I've had smoother rides over the years, but the bumps don't bother Emma at all. Which is concerning in itself. My attention splits between watching the trail, Emma, and Flossie.

A dark shape above me floats down the road about fifteen feet in front of me. It's Tawny. She flies east, following the sunrise ahead of us.

"See you there, Tawny." My words drift behind her.

In the morning light, I now see clusters of cottonwoods and poplars. On the other side of the lake, it's a sea of grass; the prairie seems to go on forever. The road curves, and now I see the lake down below. A small whitewashed cabin enclosed by, yes, a white picket fence and surrounded by trees,is beside the road. There are apple trees among the poplars, elm, and cottonwoods, their branches hanging low and heavy with fruit. The front gate is open, along with the front door of the house. Flowers and greenery fill the yard, vining and spilling over the fence and along the walls. It's a fairy tale fantasy house. All it needs is smoke curling from the chimney to make it complete.

I pull alongside the fence and park. I hear birds and the breeze in the wind trees when I turn off the bike. It sounds like home, and I'm calmer just from that. An earthy bouquet surrounds me. Whiffs of lemon balm and rosemary float by, and I see large tomatoes among the vines on the fence.

Flossie comes over to the bike with a quilt draped over her shoulder, now accompanied by a gigantic tabby. "Let's wrap your girl up and get her inside. We need to get her clothing changed, and I've got a tonic I can give her for the fever. You need to be looked at, also."

"Her name is Emma, and I'm Sellis."

My teeth are chattering, and I'm shaking as I get off the bike. Flossie hesitates and gives me a strange look when I say my name. It takes a couple of tries to make my numb fingers work, but I get my helmet off and then work on Emma's. Flossie reaches past me and lifts Spike's basket out just when I think he's going to scratch a hole in it. He leaps out onto Emma's lap with a loud meow. Emma stirs and mumbles, but her eyes stay closed.

"Oh, no. Mr. Kitty is not pleased with you!"

"Spike never hesitates to let me know what he thinks."

It's a much-needed moment of lightness, and when I look over at Flossie, we both start laughing at Spike's indignant attitude. He springs onto the front of the sidecar and starts grooming himself. Placing my hands under Emma's arms, I lift her, and Flossie wraps the quilt around her and takes her.

"We'll meet you inside." Turning around, she slowly walks away with Spike close behind.

I take a step to follow before I remember I need dry clothes for both of us. Which I'll get as soon as the tabby moves. I know I'm too good at attributing human characteristics to animals, but I swear this cat is studying me.

"I'm a good person, really. Maybe different than what you're used to, but I mean you no harm. Really. If you could put in a good word with your wolf buddy, I'd appreciate it." I reach out a hand, and she stands up and sniffs it, and gives it a nudge. "Hello to you, beautiful cat. I can't wait till Spike meets you."

Introduction complete, I pull out our bags and head into the house.

CHAPTER 21

There's a portico over the open front door with a lantern hanging down. The light from it glows on me as I stand and look inside. The sun has risen above the horizon, and I see more cottages scattered along the lake road.

Emma is on a couch wrapped in the quilt. Spike is beside her, kneading the quilt and purring. Flossie is across the open room in the kitchen, filling a teapot. "Come in, come in. I'll have tea for us shortly, and tonic for Miss Emma."

Bunches of herbs and dried flowers hang from the wooden beams of the ceiling. Potted plants sit on every available surface. It feels like home.

Emma opens her eyes when I place my hand on her forehead. "Gram, where were you? I woke up, and you were gone. I was so scared." She starts to cry, and I drop the bags and sit next to her, pulling her on my lap.

"We're fine, Em. Everything is okay." I smooth down her matted hair and wrap my other arm around her.

"Here, let's have Emma drink this." Flossie hands me a white enamel cup. " It'll help bring her fever down. You both need to get out of those wet clothes and warm up." The familiar aroma of lemon balm and honey wafts from the cup.

"How - what." She interrupts me before I get two words out. Her voice is clipped, and I know enough to shut up.

"Please. Don't dawdle. There will be time to converse."

Yes, ma'am.

Spike keeps an eye on me as I hold the cup for Emma. I help her change, and the tonic is gone by the time she's dressed and re-wrapped in the quilt.

Flossie picks up her clothes as she tells me, "There is a clothesline in the back. The sun will dry them."

Emma's eyes are drooping, and I get her and Spike comfy on the couch. "Nap a bit, and then we'll go home."

"You can change in the bathroom. Your tea will be steeping, and we can talk when you're done." Flossie stands beside a door and opens it. "The tonic will help Emma rest, and her fever should break."

I lean against the closed door and look around. Everything looks new, but it's old. Old fashioned? Is that the term I'm looking for? It's vintage, but it's not. The porcelain sink gleams, along with the yellow tile and lino-leum flooring. *What happened in the storm? What year is this? How did we get here?*

I get the feeling that Flossie (*Oh my god. Flossie.*) knows something about what happened. Okay. Time to stop dawdling as she said.

My chaps and my leather jacket are saturated. I pile my wet clothes on top of them and go back out into the main room. "Please let me help you hang these up. They weigh a ton."

"Thank you for your offer. I'll take care of them. I would like you to warm up with a cup of tea and then rest. You said your name is Sellis?" Flossie hands me a cup of tea. More lemon balm, and freshly picked. "This will refresh and calm you. What is your last name? You're not from around here, are you?"

The cup is toasty in my cold hands, and the lemon fragrance warms my heart. I can't help chuckling. "No, we're not from around here. We live west of here in Willow Banks. My name is Sellis Carlson now, but my maiden name was Weaver." I look over at her to see her reaction.

"Hmmm. Weaver, you say. I know of Willow Banks. That's quite a ways to be out on your motor contraption."

"Motorcycle," I say.

"Oh, yes. I've not seen one before. I've heard of them. Are they comfortable to sit on? Never mind, that's for another time. You need to get back to Willow Banks. Without much more delay."

"What happened to us? How did we get here? How…" I can't talk straight and find the right words to ask her what I think she knows.

She smiles at me with, I swear, affection and shakes her head. "I will tell you that it's the year 1934, and my last name is also Weaver. How you ended up here, I don't know. You shouldn't be here, though. Travelers don't go to different periods of time that I'm aware of, just places. Yes, I know that you're travelers and that we're family."

"You are my Flossie."

"Indeed. Although not how you remember me, I warrant." She laughs as she holds my cup to pour more tea into it. I remember that laugh. I can't take my eyes off her as I try to accept that this woman is real and is my grandma Flossie when she was younger than I am now.

Mind-boggling. That's the term that runs through my head.

"I'm your granddaughter. And I'm a gardener, too. Emma's my granddaughter, so she's…"

"And you both have an affinity with animals, don't you? I saw your owl at the lake, and Emma's feline companion doesn't want to leave her side. I sense an other-worldliness about Emma. She's an old soul." Flossie glances over at Emma and then back at me. "I knew someone was in trouble by the lake, and then, I knew you were family. The storm played a role in this somehow. And now, we must get you rested and back home safely."

"Will we be able to go home? I don't understand what happened at the school. The only thing I can think of is that the leaking pipe was a portal. Or else it's the water." My hands are clenched so rigid, my nails are digging into my palms.

Just breathe. I do and open my fingers.

"After the storm, we were here. Which is a totally different time. That's why I came back to find the fountain. Well, actually, Tawny, that's my owl; she led us here, because there isn't a road to the Interstate anymore. There isn't even an Interstate." I'm babbling, and my eyes are blurry.

"Shhhh. I know. I know. You are not where you should be. You need to rest as Emma is, and then we can work on getting you home." Flossie reaches over and cups my chin in her hand, and studies my face. "You carry the

Weaver family in your bones, Sellis. Promise me to learn about our family when you get home. You need to carry on our legacy. Now, sleep."

She shows me to a small room with a single bed, dresser, and chair. I'm asleep as soon as I lay down.

I sleep all day long. I don't hear a thing. I don't move. I just sleep, and when I finally wake up, it's because I hear an owl hooting. *"Tawny!"* I'm tangled in blankets and end up dragging them along with me to the open window. I can tell it's late afternoon by the light. Early owl time, but I bet Tawny has been wondering about us. "Hey, sweet pea, how are you?"

I scan the trees outside and spot her when she flies down to the fence. There's a soft tap on the door before it opens. "Are you rested? I've been hearing an owl and I think it must be yours." Flossie peers in at me from the doorway as she wipes her hands on her apron. "Jubal has been pacing for a while, so I knew there was something outside that didn't belong here."

"Who's Jubal?"

"My dog, he was with me when I found you. In fact, he is the reason I came looking for you. I heard the owl and then your voice."

It's a dog, not a wolf. Whew. One question answered. "Um. I do feel rested. How is Emma?" I head to the door as I speak, anxious to see her.

"She's still sleeping but is starting to move around, so I don't think it will be long before she wakes. Please let me show you outside so you can talk with your owl, and then we can eat and prepare for tomorrow." Turning around, she goes over to another door.

I tiptoe over to Emma and Spike. She's not hot anymore, and her color is back. The aroma of bread baking and something else - apple pie? grabs my attention. And then my stomach gurgles. I don't remember the last time I had anything to eat, but I would be willing to start with whatever smells so heavenly.

Flossie opens the back door with a smile. "First, your owl, then food."

CHAPTER 22

"Whoo. Hoot."

"Hello to you, too, Tawny." She greets me as soon as I walk out the back door into my own personal idea of paradise. How big is this yard? It goes back a long way. Apple trees, wild plums, herbs, and vegetables are mixed in with flowers. Wind rustles amongst the greenery along with bird song. It's an English Cottage Garden with a Midwestern edge. I turn in a circle and see birds and bees flitting around. Bees! I love seeing all the bees and think about my gardens and the flowers I've planted over the years to attract bees and birds. Someday my home will be like this.

I take a deep breath. Rosemary and roses. Apples, lemon balm, lavender - it's nature's potpourri out here. I run my fingers across leaves and stop to examine what I'm pretty sure is echinacea (*I know I detected that in Emma's tea.*)

I can't find Tawny in all the foliage until she hoots again.

"Hey, Sweet Pea. How amazing are you to keep up with me?" I walk over to the fence along the house. She glides down from the tree branch next to me. Her presence soothes me, and I reach out to stroke her. "Thank you for guiding us here last night. *Was that just last night? I have no concept of time anymore.* You are definitely my talisman and guide. Now, we need to get back to our time and home. First thing in the morning."

My head is clear, and my stomach is growling. The late afternoon sun is warm on my arms. I have some bruises on them, and my fingers are pretty beat up. My shoulders and neck are stiff, "Ohhh," and so are my legs. An appointment with Dr. Joel, my chiropractor, will be high on my to-do list when we get home.

I toy with the idea of switching Tawny's jesses to see if she could find her way to Caleb. No. I'm not going to take a chance on losing her. I have no idea where she could end up. Besides, we'll be home by this time tomorrow.

"Mrroww." Spike's distinctive call is accompanied by Flossie's voice. "Jubal is close behind your kitten in case your owl is skittish."

"Hoot."

I watch as Spike dashes across the yard with Jubal not far behind. Meows and barks fill the air while Tawny sits and watches it all in her zen owl way. Spike has a lot of energy to burn off, and it looks like he found the perfect playmate. Flossie comes over, carrying two cups.

"Here is more tea for you. Emma woke briefly, and her fever is gone. She drank some more tonic, but didn't want to get up. We can eat when she wakes, and I think a bath will wear her out so she'll sleep all night."

"Oh, thank you. Her mother will never let her go on a road trip with me again after this one." As I sip on my tea, I can't imagine how Lily will react to this adventure of ours. She knows Emma is safe with me. But... Things tend to go awry when Emma and I are together. I'm not sure why that is.

"You're welcome. I think we should discuss your situation while Emma sleeps. I know you must have questions, and this is perhaps a discussion best had without her," Flossie looks at me as she takes a sip.

"Why? Is there a problem? Is there something I should know? Are we in danger? Won't we be able to go home?" Questions spurt, and I spill my tea.

"No, no, I'm sorry. I didn't mean to unduly worry you." Her accent thickens, and she places a hand on my arm, steadying me. "You'll be fine. I merely meant I didn't think we wanted to talk about unknown subjects in front of a young girl. This event with you being here is something I know nothing about. I tend to think of travelers and other situations as mystifying and, therefore, inexplicable." Flossie shrugs her shoulders and holds her hands up in a gesture I've made countless times. That Lily and Emma make.

"Well, if I didn't know we were related before, I certainly do now." I laugh as I mimic her. "Please, can you tell me your story? I've been searching for my family all of my life, so finding you is, like you said, otherwordly."

"Well, as you can tell, I'm British. My family is from the county of Somerset in England. We came here to settle in Crystal Springs, along with other kinfolk and friends. We have a long history of working with the land, and we've found a good home here." She walks over to an apple tree, and after some study, picks one. As she walks back, she polishes it on her apron before handing it to me. "This tree grew from seeds my father brought from his home in Somerset."

My mind swirls. "I'm a gardener too. I have my own nursery and orchards at home in Willow Creek. No wonder it feels like home here. Your herbs and flowers and your beautiful yard. It's all so familiar and dear." I bite into the apple, and the sweet tang tastes like home, too.

Flossie smiles at me. "If your physical presence hadn't told me we were family, I would have known by your actions when you walked out here. There's magic and so much goodness in our family, Sellis, but also a bleak side and dark secrets. I believe that's why you found me and this place. Our family has been broken for years, and perhaps you and Emma can restore us."

Barks and rustling in the grass and shrubs interrupt the solemn tone, and Jubal and Spike dash past us. Tawny spreads her wings and flies off towards the lake.

"I think that's our cue to walk a bit," Flossie says.

"I would love that. There's so much to see, and I'm afraid I'm stiffening up as I stand here." I roll my shoulders and gingerly stand up. "First thing, though, what kind of apple is this?"

My hands are filled with flowers and grasses when we return. There are more flower seeds in my pockets and a promise of apples and seeds to bring home. I'm delighted at the thought of growing my own apples from the seeds of my ancestors. The complexity of that concept and how it works with time makes my head hurt - so I tuck it away.

I'm giddy. Yes. Giddy. This chance encounter has given me a sense of well-being like I've never known before. As unexpected and out-of-the-ordinary as it is, this feels right. My heart is at ease.

I learn that the cabin is at the tip of farmland owned by the Weaver family. They also have a home in Crystal Springs, which is where the rest of the family resides.

Ah. Ha. There it is, the property Seth found in the records. I wonder why this didn't show up.

The sun has set, and birdsong drifts as we walk back inside. Going over to Emma, when I touch her shoulder, she opens her eyes. "Gram! I've had the most amazing dream! I had tea with Great Grandma Flossie, and she has her own wolf. And. And. There she is. And." Her words are cut short as Jubal places his front paws on her and gives her a lick. Not to be forgotten, Spike jumps up on her legs.

She sits up, grabs Spike, and looks between Jubal, Flossie, and me. Her mouth drops, and I think this is the first time I've ever seen her speechless.

"What a great dream, huh? You look like you're feeling better, and I think your fever is gone. How about a bath, and then we'll eat and chat." I sit down next to her and wrap my arms around her, and it feels so good to laugh.

CHAPTER 23

Flossie is right. Emma didn't last long after we ate. Her fever is gone, but she's listless and sniffling. She almost fell asleep in the tub. Her brain was working just fine, though. During supper, she stopped as she took a bite and pointed her spoon at Flossie.

"Wait a minute. Your name is Flossie? Flossie what? Did you know that I have a great, great, a whole bunch of greats, grandma named Flossie? Are you named after her? Are you related to us?" Eyes wide, she looks from Flossie to me.

I'm caught off guard. Before I can sputter out a lame explanation, Emma shrugs (yes, the family shrug). "Whatever, Gram. Don't even bother. I know. I know. We'll talk later."

She continues to eat. Flossie and I avoid each other's eyes and I swallow my laughter. Thank goodness. I'm not sure about any of this. How would I explain it to Emma?

I tuck her and Spike into the bed where I slept earlier. Her eyes are half-closed, yet she continues to ask questions. "Is my jacket dry? Where are my gauntlets? How will we call Gramps? Your phone died." She plucks at the blanket until Spike head butts her, and she picks him up and snuggles him under her chin.

I bend over and kiss the top of her head and accept a sniff from Spike. "We'll make it home tomorrow. We'll be up early, so we have plenty of time. I've got this, okay? This time tomorrow, you'll be sleeping in your own bed." I fiddle with the blankets because I know how she feels. I'm anxious, too.

Spike purrs, and Emma mumbles something I can't make out. She's asleep.

Flossie has finished tidying up, and she greets me with a smile and a mug. "Let's share one more cup before you bathe and get some rest. The moon is still full, and the sky is bursting with stars."

She's right. I thought I'd seen stars before, but I can tell there aren't any man-made lights blocking their twinkles. It's dazzling. Oh. No. That tickle in my throat. My nose is stuffy. Why must I cry about everything?

I sniff and look over at Flossie. "I'm sorry. I'm going to cry because it's so beautiful here and I'm scared to death. You're so calm and serene. Why didn't I inherit any of those genes? My thoughts are whirling, and I'm afraid I'll fall apart if I stop moving."

"Please don't apologize. There's nothing wrong with the way you're feeling. This is not a normal occurrence; you're right to be anxious. But, you can also let your guard down and know that you're safe here." Flossie looks up at the sky and then back at me. "No storms tonight, a full stomach, and a safe home and family. As far as personalities, I'm a practical, common sense person. You're trying to be, but you're also ruled by your heart."

"Boy, you've got that right. My heart is right there for the world to see. But. This is totally new territory. And, I've got Emma to take care of. And Spike. I can't mess up."

She uses one of my favorite sayings on me. "You're fine. Everything will be alright."

Then we get down to business. I tell Flossie about Mom and my quest for the fountain. It's weird because I think Mom was her daughter or granddaughter. And we decided that maybe she was, but it hadn't happened yet? And that possibility would lead to profound, scientific theories that I have no desire to ponder.

"This is where I spend most of my time," Flossie says, gesturing to the cabin and surrounding land. "I love being by water of any kind, and we lived here until we built our home in town. Father farmed, and Mother and I gardened, and she passed on her knowledge of herbs and natural remedies."

"Where did she learn?" I asked.

"Her mother and her family in Britain practiced herbal arts. Coming here, we learned there are many similar plants and herbs. Learning from Mother was customary." Flossie smiles and shakes her head. "Remaining single, being self-sufficient, and encouraging wild animals to live with me, unfortunately, isn't as acceptable."

"I saw a picture of you with an owl in a book at the library."

"Ah, yes, that was Dakota. That's how I knew you were family. When I saw your owl. Winking, she continues. "The Weaver family has had travelers for generations. There must be portals or doorways around the world if they have them in England and here. Family lore tells of family members that disappeared and then returned, sometimes, years later, with fanciful stories. People thought they were delusional, touched in the head. And sometimes, they became that way because they couldn't understand what happened and couldn't cope with it."

Maybe that's what happened with Mom. She always seemed like she was searching for something. I think she was happy in the other Crystal Springs, so why did she leave there?

"I think I have even more questions now than when I left the other Springs." I roll my head around to release the tightness in my neck. "Although, I have learned so much and found Crystal Springs and you!"

"And I found you and Emma. I will always hold you in my heart."

Even though I'm beyond exhausted, I can't go to bed. This woman would have been an excellent friend and fellow adventuress. Intelligent, capable, sensitive, kind-hearted, quick-witted, she is everything I hope to be. Every once in a while, we stop talking and look at each other. And then laugh. Because, yeah. How would you explain this to someone?

I've spent another late night talking to a person from another world.

Sellis Weaver. This is your life.

Of course, morning comes too soon. Sunshine, birdsong, and a woman's voice combine to be my alarm clock. As usual, when I sleep with Emma, I wake up with no covers, and today both of her legs lay across my stomach. *How does she do that? Every time, it never fails.*

I move Emma's legs and go to the window. Flossie is picking apples. "Good morning," I call out. "That's quite the helper you have."

"She excels at keeping me company, not so much at picking up apples." Reaching down, Flossie pets Jubal. "I have apples to send home with you. You can save the seeds and grow your own."

And so our day begins. Emma seems more like her usual self, which lifts my spirits. I rearrange our bags to include Flossie's goodies. We're going home with herbs, seeds, fresh veggies, apples, plums, and more writings.

"I want you to take this home with you. It was my grandmother's and hers before. I believe you were meant to come here. Our legacy needs you." She places a worn leather-bound book with a thin braided leather band tied around it in my hands. "I've memorized much of it and copied down other parts. It's time to pass it on."

I hold it to my heart, and yes, my nose starts to tickle, and I cry. "Thank you." That's all I can say.

Leaving Flossie and Jubal is a blur. I don't want to go. And I don't know why. There's no reason to not want to go home. Why is there such a strong pull here? I busy myself with our preparations, and according to Flossie, it's only 8:00 a.m. when we leave.

"Safe journey, dear girls. I think you both should go down to the water, just to be sure." Flossie stands at the gate of her fence, and I see a tear roll down her cheek.

"Are you sure you can see through those spectacles? Oh, well. I trust your judgment. Be safe."

Emma smiles up at me. "Let's roll, Gram!" And so we do.

My last glimpse of Flossie, she has one hand on Jubal's head and is waving with the other.

We're back at the fountain in a few minutes. "Em, let's leave Spike in his basket. This won't take us long. We'll get Gramps a thermos of water and go home."

She's not sold on leaving Spike alone, but we take off our helmets and start down the hill to where the fountain/pump is.

"Hoot. Whooo."

The knot in my chest loosens. *Oh, thank you. Thank you.* Even with everything going on, I wondered where Tawny was. She glides over us as Emma responds back. "Whoo are you? Hoot! Hoot!"

"This isn't even a real fountain, Gram. How does it work?"

"Hold this right here. I'll show you." I hand her the thermos and have her hold it under the spout while I pump the handle. After a few pumps, the water spurts out.

"Is this some kind of antique? I've never seen anything like this." Emma hands me the thermos as she shakes off her hands.

"I guess it is for us, but this is what faucets started out as." Tawny hoots as she flies up to the bike. I stop and take a deep breath, and look around. I smell ozone. And we're no longer surrounded by the uncultivated, wild fields we came to. *Just so we're not in some other world. This is beginning to feel like a vicious cycle of deja vu.*

"Gram? Did it work? Are we home?" Emma steps right beside me, and her hand grasps mine as she looks around.

"I think we are. Let's go see."

CHAPTER 24

There's not a cloud in the sky when we left Flossie's and the fountain. It's a perfect day to be on the bike. Traffic is light, thanks to our early start. I wasn't paying close attention when we left Flossie's, but now I can see storm damage. It's an actual path in places through the fields that are wiped clean.

"Gram! Look!" Out of the corner of my eye, I see Emma motioning and pointing. And then I smell apple cider. An entire orchard has been demolished. A few scattered trunks stand among piles of branches and shattered trees. Apples cover the ground, and birds fly in a tasting frenzy. I'm surprised the deer haven't shown up for this treat. Although, I'm afraid this is only one of many decimated orchards.

The loss of these trees makes me cry. *What if my trees are gone? Nah. It's over a hundred miles from here.*

I guess it's the manner of storms. Extensive, yet weirdly, spotty. I'm glad the road is clear. We make good time and even take a couple of breaks to walk around.

It's close to noon when we stop at a truck stop to fill gas and have lunch. I figure I can charge my dead phone while we eat since there are charging stations at the booths for the truckers. Maybe I'll be able to get ahold of Caleb or Lily, which would be good.

"Spike and I are going to explore over there." Emma points over to the empty lot past the station. They amble off, and I drive the bike to the gas pumps.

"Mighty peculiar storms going through lately. Someone called it a derecho." The older gentleman filling up his pickup beside me is in a chatty mood.

"What is that? I've never heard that term." I put my kickstand down and give him my full attention.

"It's a newfangled word for a big windstorm. I'm seventy-three and never heard it before myself. Winds took out what was left of the town of Crystal Springs, along with the crops for miles. Not much of anything left standing over there."

All I can do is nod as he tells me more about the damage. And send up thanks to the Universe again for keeping us safe.

"Keep your eyes open, young lady. The air is heavy. I wouldn't be surprised if something else isn't brewing."

"I will, sir. You stay safe, too." He touches the brim of his hat and gives me a two-finger salute as he drives off.

I mull over what he said as I fill gas and wipe off the Trumpet. I listen to the local news over the speakers in the gas pumps. The current temp is eighty-eight with light southerly winds. No stormy weather in the forecast.

I park the Trumpet in the shade and go to put Spike in his basket.

"It's too hot for animals to stay in vehicles. I'll pretend

this is my purse." Placing the handle of the basket over her shoulder, Emma heads to the doors.

Okay. All they can do is ask us to leave.

The derecho is the topic of the hour. Our server comments on it, and I hear bits of conversation at other tables. I don't know anyone who lives here, and none of the places I hear mentioned are familiar.

My phone is plugged in and charging, and the food doesn't take long.

"Was that the storm we were in at the school?" Emma looks at me and then back at the french fry she's twirling in the plastic cup of ranch dressing.

"Uh, huh," I reply as I watch her face.

"We were," she coughs and starts over. "We were lucky we were in the school, weren't we, Gram?"

"We sure were. I always liked that old brick school. I'm glad it was built strong."

My phone gets charged to 25 percent, which should get us home. I try Caleb and Lily, but there's no service available. More derecho damage? Never one to deny my sweet tooth, we pick out half a dozen chocolate-frosted chocolate cookies for later at the counter.

"That's a pretty big purse you've got there." The woman at the till winks at me as she rings us up, and I wonder if she knows Spike is inside it. I glance over my shoulder and have a clear view of the field. "It looks like it's a perfect fit in your sidecar for all of your stuff."

"Purses, what would we do without them, right?" I laugh as I look at Emma being nonchalant with her "purse."

I place the cookies in our cooler and put our rain

suits on top of it. Just in case. There's still not a cloud in the sky, but now, I feel the heaviness in the air, too.

One last try to Caleb. Still no result. We're outta here.

⌘

The breeze stays light as we ride, but the temperature goes up. I keep an eye on the sky and do quick checks on my phone's weather app when we stop for bathroom breaks. Nothing forecast, and still no luck getting through to Caleb or Lily.

Mid-afternoon, the weather changes. I swear I feel the front move in. The wind picks up, and the temperature drops. Looking south, I see the line of clouds.

Stay calm. You've got this. Get your rain suits on. Maybe it'll miss us. But we'll be prepared.

"What are we doing? I thought you said there wasn't going to be any rain today." Emma's voice is shrill and whiny. "I hate this ugly, big yellow suit. Yellow is ugly. It feels yucky and sticky. It makes me sweat."

"I know. I feel exactly the same about mine. Here, scoot over; let's make goofy faces to match our goofy rain suits, okay?"

She's scared. I get it. I don't want to deal with more rain and another storm, either. And I so do not want to be riding my bike in one.

There was no mist, no sprinkling, it just started to rain. Those clouds rolled up to us faster than I anticipated. I don't know how many miles we rode in the rain, but I was going to ride as long as I could see.

And then the rain turned into a gray deluge. Sheets of rain pounded on us. The wind gusts were pushing at the bike, and I wondered why helmets didn't have windshield wipers on them.

It was no longer safe for us to be on the road.

Seriously? I just want to get home.

Emma is rigid as a board with her hands clenched on her seat as she stares straight ahead. I see her lips moving. She's singing to keep her courage up.

I spot an exit sign. I can't make out the name of the town, but it doesn't matter. We're in the middle of farmland, and the closest little towns are miles away. So, I do the only thing I can and pull over under the overpass.

I'm beginning to wonder if we'll ever get home.

Emma has a meltdown when we stop. "Gram, just drive. Don't stop. What if this bridge breaks and falls on us like the school did? It's not safe. We need to go home. We can go in the basement and be safe." She sobs so hard she's shaking. I wrap my arms around her and have the same fears.

"Hey, how about a snuggle with Spike? Would you be willing to sing to us? I love your songs, and they always make me feel good. None of us are happy about this rain, but we're dry here and very safe. I promise." It takes a while, and then she wipes her eyes with her hands, and reaches down and opens Spike's basket.

Spike begins to purr and climbs up into her arms. Not much is better than that.

"I think I'll make up a new song just for this particular situation," Emma announces as she settles back into the sidecar.

"Excellent plan. Here, let me wrap this around you

two. You create, and I'll be your audience." I loosely wrap the space blanket over the two of them.

Emma sings and keeps up a running commentary. I ask a question now and then or comment on the latest lyrics. My thoughts race along at top speed. When will this end? It hasn't cleared up enough to be comfortable taking off. A few vehicles have gone past, but no one else has taken shelter here. I guess if I wasn't on a bike, I'd keep going too. A big ol' white caddy cruises by with two older couples in it. Two men in front, two women in the back. They all peer out the windows at us, and the guy in the passenger seat shakes his head. I'm thinking he's not a motorcycle enthusiast.

This is the most peculiar weather. It shows up out of nowhere, and there is no end to it.

Wait a minute. Everything feels kinda strange. I try to remember the name of the town on the sign and can't. Even the truck stop, what town was that? Something is off, but I don't know what.

Shake it off, woman. We're fine. You're just jittery from the storm.

I pull out my phone to see if I can get the weather on it. I just hope it's missed Willow Creek, so I don't have to deal with a flooded road.

Ha. I'll cross that bridge when I come to it.

"Whooo. Whoo."

Can it be? I think it is.

"Tawny? Where are you?"

And here she is. As bedraggled and sodden as we are. But she's safe under the overpass with us. She descends onto the front of the sidecar and definitely looks owly. Ha. Ha.

I feel better about things now that Tawny is here. How weird is that? "Hey, I think it's cookie time. I'm ready for some chocolate, how bout you? I wish I had a mouse snack for Tawny." I take a bite of one and hand Emma another one. Neither Tawny nor Emma react to my mouse comment. Tawny sits stoically on the sidecar facing the rain, and Emma sings between bites.

"Ahhh. Chocolate makes everything better." I lean against the Trumpet and watch the rain fall as I chew.

CHAPTER 25

Tawny spreads her wings and takes off into the rain. She's effortless and silent - and then she's gone. What changed? What did she hear? Smell? I don't see anything different. Plus, she went back the way we came from. Why?

"Hey, Tawny, where'd you go?" Her abrupt departure shakes me out of my numbness. It feels like we've been here for hours, but it's barely been one when I check my phone.

"Emma, why don't you guys get up and stretch your legs?" I motion her over.

"Does Spike need his leash?" She asks.

"I don't think Spike is going to run off into this rain." I walk over to the edge of the overpass, and I can see down the road. The rain is letting up. It's no longer a wall of gray. I reach over and pet Spike, who is snuggled up on Emma's shoulder.

"He's really become a shoulder cat on our trip, hasn't he?" I chuckle as his purrs intensify, and he pushes his head into my hand.

It's almost like Tawny knew the rain was ending when she left. But where did she go?

"The rain is done. Let's go, Gram. Hurry before it starts again." Emma looks up at me, and I see the worry in her eyes. "Please?"

"Yep, I agree. Let's get this show on the road," I give her a thumbs up.

We're packed and on the road in no time. In our rain suits.

"Why? It's not raining anymore. I feel like a giant Peep." Emma even manages to pout, which I haven't seen her do in years.

"I like Peeps. I think they're cute," is my response as I start the Trumpet.

Clouds fill the sky and roll and rumble past us. Lightning strikes flash occasionally. The ditches are filled with water, and in places, it covers the road. It's a slow and deliberate ride; there will be no hydro-planing today. Traffic is back to normal now that the rain is over. I study the countryside as we get closer to home. I should start seeing familiar landmarks now; we've only got about fifty miles to go.

We stop at a rest area before we hit the home stretch. There were some frantic hand motions from the sidecar, and it took me a while to figure out what Emma was doing. When I remembered the "shaking letter t" means toilet, I realized I was ready for a bathroom break, too. It's good to stretch and clear my head.

My phone is almost dead again, and I still can't reach Caleb or Lily.

"Just text 'em, Gram, and tell them we're on our way.

And ask Mom if we can have pizza for supper. I'm starving for pizza." Emma instructs me as she gets herself and Spike situated.

I don't tell her my texts come back with an error message that I'm sending them to an invalid number.

That little voice is getting louder. The one saying something's wrong.

The miles slip by. I don't see storm damage here, just standing water from the recent rainstorm. The sun is out, and I regret keeping our rain suits on. We are a rolling sauna.

I almost miss the exit because the sign for my nursery is gone. The sign, Wind Trees Nursery, that tells me I'm only five miles from home. It's been there for years now.

What is going on? Did they take it down? There's the exit, but where's my sign?

The tiny knot of uneasiness in my stomach growls at me. Something is off. There's no reason my sign would have been taken down. It doesn't even look like there was ever a sign there.

"Where's our sign?" Emma looks at me and then over her shoulder when we stop at the exit. "How come you took it down?"

" I don't know why it's gone," I respond. I'm spooked, and I know something is wrong. I sit at the stop sign and try to sort through the various scenarios and possibilities zooming through my thoughts. My fingers tap the grips, and I'm biting my lower lip.

Breathe, Sellis. Breathe deep. I've got this. I can figure this out.

Okay. Time for something physical. We're pulled

over far enough at the stop sign to get off and get rid of these rain suits. We'll cool down and move a little, and I will find my zen place so Emma doesn't freak out.

I turn off the bike and say, "Okay, time to be plain ol' bikers. Hop out, and let's get these Peep suits, I mean, rain suits, off."

She grins at me as she unbuckles her seat belt and gets out. "Thank you, thank you, thank you."

I'm not as zen as I could be, but a big hug before we start back soothes us both. I don't have answers, but I'll figure it out.

I turn south to go where home should be.

There's a general sameness to the countryside as I drive. But. Again, there's something off. How can orchards disappear? Were there always so many sunflower fields along here? And houses. Where is the Green's house? What is that development?

What is happening? What is going on?

We go across the Willow River, which is quite high, and turn onto Willow Road.

There's no sign pointing the way to my nursery.

The rows of wind trees line the driveway, but that's not my mailbox. And my grass is never that high.

I turn in and stop a few yards down the road. My heart soars at the sight of my beloved poplars, cotton-woods, elms, and various pines, with the row of lilacs and dogwoods in front. Emma tries to talk over the bike. She's close to shrieking. "Gram. What is going on? This is not home. I thought it was. Where are we? Where is my mom? Why are," she bursts into tears.

My mind is blank. For what seems like forever, I don't

have any words to respond to her. I don't know how to fix this.

Fortunately, my numbness is fleeting, and I find my Grandma superpowers before we're both sobbing uncontrollably.

I bend down and flip up her visor. I put my hand under her chin and turn her face so she's looking at me. Her tear-soaked face breaks my heart. "Em, we're okay. I think the storm has made connections between the different worlds wacky. You're right. It doesn't seem like this is home, but we'll check it out."

Her sobs slow down enough so she can talk. "How come you didn't know this is the wrong world?"

Good question. I can think of dozens of hints now when I sit here and think back over today. There isn't any one detail that stands out, but I ignored so many little things. Names of towns that I didn't recall, no familiar landmarks or houses along the way... especially once we got closer to home.

Suck it up, Buttercup. And breathe.

"I don't know what happened, Em. I promise I'll figure it out, and we'll get home." I grab a tissue from my jacket and wipe her face, blow her a kiss, and we go down the driveway.

My house is gone. The trees are here, but not my orchards. There aren't any greenhouses or outbuildings, just a garage, and a tiny shop. In fact, this place looks like the original place I bought years ago. The bones of what I built from are here, but this isn't my home.

There's the creek. I know the twists and curves it takes like the back of my hand. *What is going on?*

A border collie comes bouncing down the road. I hear barks over the engine because I'm driving as slow as I can so that I regain my composure. I need to figure out what I'm going to say.

We follow the road to the front of the house. The border collie twirls and barks beside us. "Baily. Stop. Come here." A man is sitting on a bench watching us. The dog runs over to him, and I pull up and stop.

"Hello!" I take off my helmet as I get off the bike. "Emma, just wait here, okay?"

"Hello to you. How can I help you?" The dog has come over to the sidecar and is checking Emma out. The man follows.

"Well, I'm lost. I was looking for a place called Wind Tree Nursery, but this is not it." I walk over to him and hold out my hand. "I'm Sellis Carlson, and this is my granddaughter, Emma. We're on a back-to-school trip."

"I'm Joe. My wife's at work, and I'm waiting for her to get home." He says. "I don't know of any nursery out here. There are some tree farms west of us but no nurseries."

"I think we're going to head into town and check into our motel. I goofed up somehow. You have a beautiful place here. I love all of your trees."

We talk about the location, and he gives me directions to town. I keep it brief because I don't know what I would say if he started asking questions.

"I'm sorry we popped in on you. Thanks for the directions. Enjoy your evening." Helmet and gloves on, I smile down at Emma as we drive away.

I blink back tears as I drive down the familiar road.

At the end of the driveway, when I stop, I look down at Emma. "We're going to get a motel room and have some pizza. Then we're going to get some sleep, and tomorrow we're going back to the fountain."

The roads and layout of this Willow Banks are similar to mine. We drive by the tree farms Joe mentioned. There are so many details that are different. At least the road to town is the same. I smile as we drive past the shelter belt where Tawny's nest was. It's still there! But that reminds me that I hadn't seen her since she flew off when we were at the overpass.

An inexpensive chain motel that allows pets is next to a pizza place (Yay!) at the edge of town.

"Can we please have half pepperoni and half Hawaiian pizza?" Emma asks as soon as I turn off the bike.

"Of course, you can. I didn't know there was any other kind."

Full of pizza and clean and relaxed after a soak in the tub, Emma and Spike are tucked into bed. She's subdued and isn't her usual vivacious self. She avoids my questions and comments. "I don't want to talk about this. I just want to be home. Can I read for a while? Then I'm going to sleep so I can wake up and go home." She picks up her book and makes a point of concentrating on it.

"Okay, sweet girl. I'm going to take a shower. We'll talk in the morning. I love you. Sleep tight." I bend over and kiss her forehead. Spike is sprawled across the pillow next to her, and I reach over and stroke him. "I'll leave the bathroom door cracked in case you need something, and then I'll be in this other bed."

No response.

That's okay. She's scared and upset.

Me, too.

After my shower, I grab my backpack and fully charged phone. I try Caleb and Lily again, even though I know what the result will be.

Emma's asleep, so I put her book on the nightstand and turn off the lamp. *I promise we'll get home. I promise.*

My anxiety is flaring now that we've stopped moving. I pull out my journal and start to list my thoughts. I set it down and go through the papers and books I got from Anne, Grace, Seth, and Flossie.

If I was delusional and none of this was real, I wouldn't have all this stuff, right?

I hope I find something to explain why we're going to these different worlds and can't get home. The only solution I've come up with is to go back to the fountain in Crystal Springs and try again. I know there are other places like it, but we never talked about where they are. I skim through the books and papers, but nothing pops out at me. I smile as I recall the comfortable sense of belonging I had at both Crystal Springs.

In another exercise in futility, I try my sister's number. Same result.

Ah, how about the phone book. Yeeks. This is a bit unnerving. The phone prefixes are all different. Some of the same street names and businesses, but enough unknown ones to remind me that this isn't my Willow Banks.

I'm exhausted. But I'm grateful that we're safe and warm and not caught in a storm somewhere. Again. I'm also thankful that my credit card and money work in all these different worlds. That would be… I can't even think about it.

I thank the Universe for this adventure's positives and ask for guidance tomorrow to help us get home.

Before I turn off my lamp, I look over at Emma, who is now sprawled sideways on her bed. *Oh, yeah, and I'm thankful I have my own bed to sleep in.*

CHAPTER 26

"Sellis! There is another path you can take to get home. Look in our book."

Flossie's voice wakes me. The alarm clock reads 3:17 a.m. Is it a dream? Or something else?

The book.

I'm awake.

I get up and grab my sweatshirt from the foot of the bed. As I pull it on, I step over to Emma. She's wrapped up in her blankets with Spike curled up beside her pillow. I place my hand on her forehead, which feels just fine. She's not congested and no longer feels warm. Thank goodness.

The moon shines between the two curtains over the window, and there's enough light for me to walk across the room. Once there, I turn on the lamp and grab my backpack. I rummage through it, feeling for the worn leather book. When I hold it in my hand, I sense Flossie so strongly, it takes my breath away. And it's as though she shares some much-needed strength with me. Here in the night's darkest time, every one of my fears and inadequacies has come to the surface.

I'm scared. What am I going to do? What am I doing wrong? Why can't we get home? Okay. The first thing I will do is stop this line of thinking. I am not doing anything wrong. I wonder if the storms are somehow affecting the gateways between the worlds. We just have to keep trying until we find our world again. Let's see what Flossie wants me to see.

This is not merely a book. It's a family history. Recipes, sketches, letters, dried flowers and leaves, maps. It's a treasure. And it's daunting but exhilarating as I skim through the pages. I have to remind myself to scan and just glance.

I look forward to the time when I can curl up and savor each and every page.

And there it is.

Doorway - McDowell Lake.

McDowell Lake? McDowell Dam? My McDowell Dam? No way. That's like, five miles from my house.

A journal entry written by Lizzie Weaver, who I assume is Flossie's mother, tells of a peculiar incident along the northwestern portion of McDowell Lake. On a family outing, she explored with Flossie while her husband was fishing. The two of them discovered a natural spring and stopped to explore it. They drank the water and had the same experience Emma and I did. Lizzie figured out what happened (apparently, they went to a pristine, unsettled area), and they returned to their original site. There's a hand-drawn map with the directions, and it looks like it's off the current hiking path at the dam.

Huh. That's interesting. It's another option, right? I wonder where it would take us today. And do I dare try? What if we go back in time again?

I'm pretty sure the storms are causing problems with the doorways. Now that the weather has settled down, I believe we should be able to get home.

If we get on the road at about 7 a.m., and our only stops are gas and bathroom breaks, we can get back to the springs in about three hours. Go to the fountain, the water, and turn around. I have to believe it will work right. My phone is fully charged, I'll call Caleb, and I'll know right away if it goes through.

It'll work. It has to. What if it doesn't? What if we end up wandering around into more unknown worlds? Enough. It'll work. This time tonight, we'll be home. And if we can't get home from the springs, we'll find the spot at McDowell Lake.

∽

Here I am, dressed, with the complimentary mini-pot of coffee finished. And it's barely 6 a.m. I've come up with a plan and fine-tuned it after I tried to fall back asleep. Unsuccessfully. At least Emma and Spike slept. Now comes the tricky part. Reminding Emma that we're having an adventure. And not letting my fear show.

"Hey, bright ray of sunshine, time to wake up." I plop onto Emma's bed and work on unraveling the sheets and blankets wrapped around her.

"Mrprh." The muffled response doesn't sound pleased. Which means it's tickle time. Fortunately, she's still ticklish. Not happy, though.

"Okay, here's the plan. We'll try the stuffed french toast and a huge glass of chocolate milk and either a banana or a nectarine." I ramble on as I get up and finish packing. "I'm curious about what you put on french toast stuffed with a special surprise. Something involving choc- olate. What do you think? And then, we're going to try our hand at becoming Iron Butts."

"Gram! What did you just say?" Arms flailing and sheets flapping, Emma sits up and scoots to the edge of the bed. "What is an iron butt? It sounds gross. Is it like armor?" She's found the clothes I laid out for her and is scrutinizing my choices. "Are you positive about the french toast? I don't think maple syrup will work, but maybe chocolate syrup would?"

"We'll see. Where's Spike's leash? I can take him out- side while you finish up, and then we can eat, and I'll tell you our plan for today." Spike is still wrapped inside the sheets and has decided we're playing "attack the human hands."

"No, wait, let me come with. I don't want to stay alone." Clothes in hand, she stands still and looks at me. "Please?"

Of course, she doesn't want to be alone. I'm glad she's talking to me and not giving me the silent treatment anymore.

I stand up and reach over to hug her. "Perfect. I need all the help I can get to deal with this wild cat."

Emma is not sold on the 'Iron Butt' concept. Being nine years old and literal, she's not totally convinced that she'll still have a flesh butt when we're done.

"We're not going to be real 'Iron Butt' riders, Em. They ride a thousand miles in one day." She's following Spike as I pack the bike. "We don't have a thousand miles to go, only about two hundred each way. But, we aren't going to take our time on our stops. We'll get gas and do bathroom breaks and then ride."

"Oh. I get it. Our butts will be sore because we're riding for hours."

"Exactly. but it'll be worth it because we'll be home early tonight." We smile at each other. She holds up her empty hand and crosses her fingers. I hold up both hands with crossed fingers.

The stuffed french toast is a decadent, over-the-top way to begin the day. I am now caffeinated enough to get us two hundred miles without gasoline.

Once again, we ride into the rising sun, and a calm, late summer morning. I remember why I love riding. Traffic is light. I smell apples and newly harvested grain. The sunshine on the fields and trees along the highway highlights the autumn color schemes. I swear there are millions of sunflowers welcoming the morning sun, and they put a smile on my face that lasts for miles.

Our first stop is at a rest area.

"Hoot. Hoot," greets us when we come outside and go back to the Trumpet.

"Tawny!" We exclaim together. She peers down at us from a tree.

"I was so worried she was lost." Emma looks between Tawny and me. "Were you, too?"

"I was," I admit. "Tawny has a magical knack of find-ing us, though, doesn't she?" A weight is lifted from my heart as I look at Tawny. "We're headed to the fountain. Meet us there, okay, sweet pea?"

The miles pass quickly. I do not plan to ever take part

in a real "Iron Butt" ride. I am thankful for the padding that I have while I'm on the subject of butts.

And here we are at the Crystal Springs exit. The school is gone here, too. I look down at Emma as we ride past. Her hands are fists, and she's biting her bottom lip. *I understand totally, Em.*

It's uncanny. The landscape by the fountain looks so much like ours. Similar trees and overgrown brush. The lake even looks the same. And there's the fountain. I pull over and turn off the bike.

"Let's do this." I get off and then help Emma and Spike. We hold hands as we make our way down the hill. Spike even behaves, only pouncing on grasshoppers when we reach the fountain.

"We'll turn on the water together, okay?" I look at Emma, and then a familiar sound makes both of us look up. And, there's Tawny.

"Who are you?" Emma sings out as we flip up the handle, and the water gushes out.

I smell ozone, and a tingle goes down my spine. And then I hear my phone. It's Caleb's ring tone.

It worked. We're home.

CHAPTER 27

The miles fly by, and I swear I don't speed. Too much.

I've driven on this highway for years, and I see familiar houses and farm buildings as we drive by. They're part of the scenery as we travel through the state. Why didn't I listen to my gut yesterday when we came through here? Part of me knew something was wrong. Whatever. We are back where we belong. Finally.

We're going home.

My cheeks hurt from smiling so much. Not just smiling, I'm beaming.

I glance down at Emma, and she looks up at me with a gigantic grin on her face. She gives me a double thumbs up and then points down the road with both forefingers.

"Take me Home, Country Roads" Drat. I can't get that refrain out of my head. Yes, please, take us back to the place we belong.

One last stop for gas and bathroom breaks, and we'll be home. "Emma, call your mom. I've got a bunch of texts and missed calls from her. You can talk to her while you let Spike out."

"Mom is at your place; I told her we're almost home."

Emma puts the phone on the seat. "She said Gramps was ready to drive and get us."

Oops. I guess I should've kept trying to actually talk to him instead of just leaving a text.

I hit auto-dial and breathe.

"On my way! That's it? Where. Are. You. Are you okay?"

"I'm sorry. It's a long, crazy story, and I…"

The silence is louder than his words. I know the exact expression on Caleb's face, and I appreciate the effort he's making to remain unruffled. I would've been going crazy if the roles were reversed.

"We'll be home in about an hour. I just filled gas, and we're headed back out. We're fine. Have you seen Tawny today? Oh, good." I walk over to Emma and Spike and point back to the bike.

"Okay. I love you, too. Yep, I'll tell her. See you soon." I put the phone in my pocket and zip it up. "Love from Gramps. Let's go home."

"They sound mad, Gram." She pays very close attention to getting Spike settled.

"Nah, they're not mad. Worried and upset, but we can understand that, right?" I wrap my arms around her and turn her around. "We would feel the same if we didn't hear from them. It's all good now. We're gonna be home soon!"

"Okay, Gram, let's roll."

I'm elated. This is my driveway. I know every bump and turn. These are my trees. My creek. My dogs. My cats. My house. My husband, daughter, and granddaughter.

My world.

The End

ACKNOWLEDGMENTS

I am grateful for the encouragement, guidance and support I found as I wrote this story.

My heart is filled with thanks to so many.

Gitzie, we wrote a story about a grandma and her beloved granddaughter who have adventures on Grandma's magical motorcycle. You were nine that summer. And so it began.

Kerry, my husband, fellow porch sitter, and creek-side enthusiast. Your pride in me is humbling, and your love surrounds me.

The Dakota Writers welcomed me, listened to me, and believed in my words. They were the first people I discovered that didn't love me and have to read my words. Sonvy Sammons sat beside me, and I still feel her encouraging me.

My online critique group, The WordSisters, have been my writing and reading partners since 2017. I found them through the writing organization WFWA. I appreciate all that I have learned and continue to learn from them.

Gayle Schuck, Norma Nichols, Connie Volk, and Andra Marquardt - my local writers group. You are honest and kind, along with being my human dictionaries and grammar police. All while believing in my words. I cherish the bond we've developed.

Harriett Davis, Gayle Schuck, and Julie Henderson proofread and edited my manuscript.

Lynn Prouty - we have brainstormed and shared our words once a month for years. So different, yet all from the heart.

Carrie of *cheekycovers.com* built my website and magically transformed my fountain picture into a piece of art for my cover. Your talent and your patience are super powers.

Miranda Stanley, my bonus daughter - Thank you for making the time to take pictures for my author's website and book. You did a marvelous job, and I didn't even have to sit on my hands.

To all of my furry kids who walked across my keyboard, plopped upon my desk and my feet, and distracted and supported me in their unique ways through this process - your spirits are part of each and every page.